MW00326034

THE VENOM
PROTOCOLS

The Venom Series | Book 1

JOHN MURRAY MCKAY

ISBN 978-1-7362075-5-0

Corvus Quill Press LLC
901 S. 2nd St. Ste. 201
Springfield, Illinois 62704

www.corvusquillpress.com

To Bonnie, Sue, Michelle, Jessica and Juli. Thank you for being fans and carrying me all these years. I love you all.

CHAPTER ONE

July 04, 2015. North Beach, Oahu.

My hands rested softly on the weathered railing, a finger tracing patterns on the fading varnish of the outside deck as I looked out over the ice-blue expanses of the mighty Pacific Ocean. It was late afternoon, and most of the surfers had already come in to get ready for the night's Fourth of July celebrations. A few tourists still lingered in the surf, taking in the last rays of the tropical sun before it finally faded away. I watched with detached attention as they slowly made their way back to the hotels and the evening dinner, laughing happily as they went.

Running my hand through my long brown hair, I could still smell the seawater from my earlier swim. It lingered on my fingertips, a smell of paradise and a world away from who I used to be. The island of Oahu in Hawaii had become my home, though I never saw myself truly as a citizen of any country. I was simply a name on a passport, a face you instantly forgot as soon as you turned your head.

Like I never existed.

With the hotel lights slowly coming to life in the distance and the evening luau fires being stoked, I turned and headed back inside. Smiling at the still and naked form of Katherine lying on my bed, I bent down and kissed the nape of her suntanned neck. Her breathing was rhythmic and shallow as the ceiling fan cooled and lapped at her hot skin. She worked the local surf shop and was one of the few people I allowed near me. I liked her company, both as a friend and a lover, but she never asked about my past. To her, I was simply Charlie O'Donnell, an artist who decided to move away from the mainland to pursue her career in Hawaii. I adored Katherine, and we could talk for hours on end, laughing about the world and all the wonderful things in it. But she could also see when I grew quiet and the old memories came back to me. Katherine would hold me tight as we sat on the steps of the beach house and watched the flowing blue waves of the Pacific, melancholic and enigmatic in its ways. Maybe the world made more sense out here, maybe it was a place where I could breathe and be free again. Shaking my head and hearing the rustling of bedsheets as the twenty-five-year-old stirred and sighed deeply and contently, I headed over to an unfinished painting and settled down by the easel. It didn't matter that I wasn't the world's best painter; there was a release and inner peace in my work, the vivid watercolors dancing across the once blank canvas. The power to just let go and be myself for once, no pretending. I did not have to be Mary Suratt, Khioniya Guseva, Charlotte Corday, Valerie Solanas, or Violet Gibson. I could simply be Charlie.

That was all I wanted.

You should have burnt those passports, I thought sullenly to myself, brushing a stroke of red paint across the canvas. Old habits die hard, I guessed. As hard as I tried, I could never bring myself to destroy those damned things. Maybe it was a safety net of sorts; perhaps it was a paranoia that my past would eventually catch up to me. One did not just walk away from such a bloodied and storied history and not expect retribution along the way. How many lives did I destroy, how many families ripped apart? Did it even help to remember their names and faces, or were they simply numbers inside brown manila envelopes?

No, they were simply pieces on a chessboard, removed at the order of some shadowy hand behind the scenes. They never got their pretty, manicured hands dirty, were never there when the bloody knife dropped. Cowards, every single one of them. I sat back in disgust, my mood for painting ruined.

There was many a sleepless night where I would lie awake and think of the past and hate myself all over again. Would that woman I left behind in the burnt-out factory shell in New York ever really leave me? Could we ever be truly separated?

Shut up Charlie, just shut up, I scolded myself, getting up and walking to the open door, needing fresh air to think again. Stopping for a moment, I sniffed the evening air and shook my head in disbelief. He stunk of cheap cologne and the perfume of the stewardess he had banged on the flight over. Whoever he was, he was good, or maybe I was losing my edge. Either way, he was in my private space, and I didn't appreciate it at all. Katherine slowly sat up in bed, short blond hair tussled and eyes still red.

"What's going on?" she mumbled, only seeing the shape of the man in the corner.

"Sweetie, get dressed and I will see you at Germaine's in half an hour. Off you go." It wasn't a tone I often used with her, but she recognized it immediately and scampered to get her clothes strewn across the floor. With a quick peck on the cheek and a final look back, she quickly exited the beach house and disappeared into the night. When she was finally gone, I pulled a chair around and focused my attention on the stranger. He was just under middle age, not overly handsome, but the signs of working in an office clearly reflected in him, the hands smooth from working a desk too long.

"I thought I smelled pig. Whatever the agency you work for wants, you've come to the wrong place. Get back on that plane and I'll let it be; nobody needs to get hurt here."

The man simply smiled and sat forward with his hands crossed. "I must say, it took some effort to track you down here; you covered your tracks very well indeed. Luckily, a retired station chief here on the island recognized your photo from an old dossier and put the call through to HQ. You look good for a woman who died three years ago in Sydney. There was not even a red flag on one of your old passports, which was impressive," he said, flicking back a lock of black hair.

"Spit it out, pig. My girl is waiting for me, and you are cutting into my drinking time. What do you want?" I slowly reached for a pen laying on the table, twirling it between my fingers, never taking my eyes off the man.

"The agency which I represent was most impressed with the work you did in Colombia and Northern Ireland, and we want to bring you out of your so-called retirement. Just this time, your unique talents will be used in service of the government."

"I'm not the person you think I am," I replied, knowing that my bluff would fail.

"Please. Let us dispense with these childish charades; you are not fooling anyone." He flipped open a hefty dossier and proceeded to scan through it. "Over fifty confirmed hits that we know of. My word, you have been busy . . .Charlie, is it? The thing is, organized crime has grown wild over these last few years, and the time has come to trim back the weeds so to speak."

"Why me?" I asked, the suspicion and derision sitting shallow in my voice.

"The government and agency which I represent cannot have any direct involvement in such sanctions on citizens of the United States, so we felt you would be an ideal fit for our plans."

"I'm not interested. Take your things and go. I am not that person anymore."

"Oh, you don't have a choice in the matter. If you want your idyllic life to continue here on the island, you'll do us this favor. Failing that, we know of at least thirty individuals and four foreign governments that would pay handsomely to know of your whereabouts, and it would be a personal tragedy for you if we leaked that information to—" He never had the chance to finish his sentence. My hand was a blur as the pen streaked across the room and embedded itself deeply in his forehead. His eyes went wide with shock before he slumped forward from the chair and fell to the floor. I lifted him up by his now bloody collar and looked him deeply in the eyes.

"Damn you for doing this; damn you," I raged between

clenched teeth, knowing that my life on the island was over. I had been compromised, and I had maybe twenty minutes tops before this place would be swarming with government agents.

Move, Charlie, move. There was no time to waste, and every moment counted. I ripped the back of the painting open and removed a stack of dollar bills and two unused British passports from the back. Grabbing a nearby bugout bag with extra clothing and supplies, I headed to the kitchen and ripped out the main gas line before lighting a packet of matches. With one last look over my shoulder, I left my life behind, the glow of the burning beach house lighting up the streaks of tears running down my face.

I had to find Katherine and get off the island as soon as possible. All hell was about to be unleashed, and I had no choice but to run again. Run and hope these bastards didn't find me again. Was it too much to ask to live in peace? Too much to be left alone? To be happy again?

Don't think, just run. There is still time for you to get away. Run and never look back.

But even as I raced across the dark sand with the sounds of fire engines howling in the distance and a burning building behind me, I knew the bitter truth was staring me squarely in the face. My demons were alive and well, and they were coming for me again.

Charlie O'Donnell is dead. My name is Charlotte Corday. I am an assassin.

CHAPTER TWO

How could I have been so careless? The thoughts raced through my mind as I sped along the deserted beach. *Everything was perfect till they found me again.* It didn't matter to me who they were or what they wanted from me; all that was important was getting as far away from here as possible. Luckily, it wasn't far to Germaine's, but the streets were clogged with tourists that came down for the Independence Day long weekend. It was easy for me to get lost between the chaos of drunken frat boys and screaming children pointing at fireworks while their overweight parents snapped photographs every two seconds. It also gave me time to think and get my head straight again. *The airport will be swarming with agents by the time we get there, and they will be on the lookout for us. No, we will have to find another way off the island. I still have some contacts left over on the mainland I can use though.* Biting my lip, I pushed through the crowd lining the streets who were happily waving oversized American flags. Something made me look over my shoulder, maybe years of training and instinct, but I saw the figures in dark suits appear behind me, silent and deadly. They were already a step ahead of me, anticipating my next move.

Deciding to get off the main street, I ducked into a back street, heading down the dark and trash-filled alley, every sound amplified tenfold, every little noise a betrayal of my escape. I caught their presence a split second before they came at me; two agents materialized from the shadows, the full moon glinting off their standard issue Berettas.

Disarm. Disable. Escape.

They never had a chance to use their sidearms as I took the first agent down with a palm strike to the throat, crushing his larynx instantly. As he lay writhing in pain on the ground, I sensed the second agent behind me, blocking an overhead strike and drilling my elbow into his solar plexus.

Short, sharp blows; don't let him breathe. Move, move. The words rang through my mind and I stayed on him, making sure every hit counted, driving him backwards against the alley wall. As he slumped to his knees, I cracked him squarely on the jaw with the Beretta, knocking him out cold. It was over in seconds, before they could even react. Checking the magazine on the service weapon, I tucked it into my belt before quickly escaping the chocking confines of the alley, leaving behind a trail of destruction. There was no time for emotion or sentiment, just another mission to complete.

God, will you listen to yourself, Charlie? This is everything you said you'd left behind, that you swore you'd never become again. I could hear the sounds of police sirens behind me. The net was pulling tighter, cutting off my escape with every second I wasted.

Stow the monologue and move your ass. We're almost there. I lucked out as Germaine's was only a twenty-minute brisk walk away. As usual, the place was packed with tourists, with a few locals milling around. Pushing through the laughing and obviously drunk mob, I desperately searched for Katherine. *Where are you? Where are you?* I kept thinking to myself, desperation growing by the second. Finally, I spotted her standing by the cocktail bar, mai tai in hand. She smiled and ran to embrace me, but I pushed her gently away.

"What's going on?" I hated seeing the worry in her soft green eyes, the fear that something was about to go wrong. I knew that look; I had seen it too many times in my life.

"I haven't got time to explain, but you have to come with me. If there's ever been a time to trust me, now would be it. We have to go; please, Katherine." Maybe it was the look she had never seen in my eyes, maybe there was something in me that made her trust me; I was not sure, but I grabbed her hand and ran to the nearby parking lot.

"Give me a second." I leapt into a stationary old model Jeep and pulled a handful of wires out from under the steering wheel. It was nothing to hot-wire the vehicle, and soon we set off down the highway to the harbor. Keeping an eye on the road and for any possible pursuers, I noticed Katherine shivering in the passenger seat, despite the warm evening air. "Listen, there are some people coming for me and I have to leave, but I can't force you to come with me. If you want, I'll drop you somewhere safe and come back for you when this is all over."

She bit a lock of her blonde hair and looked at me intently, her green, catlike eyes shimmering with tears. "What do they want with you?" she asked, crossing her arms tightly.

"They want me to hurt people again, and I would rather run than ever do that again. I made a promise to myself to never go back to that life, and dammit, I'm going to keep it! You need to keep out of sight for a few days, at least till it's safe. I'm not sure if they know about you."

Katherine looked out over the moonlit Pacific Ocean and then back at me, taking my hand in hers. "The safest place in the world is right next to you." She laid her head on my shoulder as I reached behind me and placed a jacket over her still shivering body. There was no going back for us now. The Jeep roared into the unknown night, carrying the two passengers safely inside.

Half an hour later, we reached the Kaneohe Yacht Club. The place was relatively quiet, barring one or two distant parties on the go, as I pulled the Jeep in. I doubted anyone would bother us; the harbormaster would have clocked out for the night and the partygoers would be too drunk to take any notice of us. My biggest worry was the US Coast Guard out on patrol, but I'd evaded them before so it should not be that much of a challenge. I kept a small sailing boat fueled up for weekend expeditions at the end of the quay, and we soon boarded.

"Go check the radio and supplies; I don't want to stay here any longer than we need to." I smiled at Katherine and hugged her tightly. "Everything's going to be okay, I promise."

She nodded, trying her best to be brave before heading belowdecks. If we hurried, we could make the outer lying islands before sunrise and refuel there before making a run to Japan. I had planned for this eventuality a thousand times in my head, rerunning the escape plan till it was second nature to me.

No time for emotion; follow the protocols. Don't think; react. I had hoped this day would never come, that I would finally be left alone to live my days in peace. Maybe it was a delusion, a false hope that those bastards would never find me again, never drag me back into the blood-soaked nightmare of my past.

I should have kept moving, never stopping. Got too comfortable here; lost my edge. I angrily cast off the mooring line before turning back to the boat. "Katherine, you ready to go?" I called out, but there was no response from below deck. Cautiously, I moved across the deck, reaching for a carefully hidden Glock in a nearby cooler box. Every sense was on ragged edge, waiting for the inevitable penny to drop.

"Katherine?" I called out again. A shuffling of footsteps and the sounds of crying reached my ears.

"I'm sorry, Charlie. They were waiting for me downstairs." Streaks of black mascara ran down her freckled face as a gunman in black stepped out behind her, Berretta aimed squarely at her back while three more agents appeared from the shadows.

Calmly, I raised the Glock toward him, fighting to keep my rapidly racing heartbeat under control. Had to keep it together now, assess the situation, and take appropriate action.

"We had hoped to discuss this rationally. Now you've forced us into this," the agent hissed, finger dancing precariously over the trigger. "It's simple, Miss Corday. Do us this one favor and we will leave you in peace and quiet. Are you in or out?"

Disarm. Disable. Escape.

A single shot rang out.

My name is Charlotte Corday.

I was an assassin for the Italian Mafia.

This is the story bathed in blood and tears of the woman the FBI called "the most dangerous human being on the planet."

I am codename: Venom.

CHAPTER THREE

23 May 1980. New York City.

The age of the gentleman gangster, of the great mob bosses of the past was over. The memories of the elite Cosa Nostra—of Genovese, Masseria, and Costello—had faded away into folklore and hearsay to be told by old Mafioso to their grandchildren around the dinner table. New York was a goddamn zoo, and the streets ran red with blood. Gangs like the Dirty Ones and the Nomads had turned Brooklyn into their own private war zone while the authorities looked on helplessly. Maybe they just didn't want to do anything. Half of New York's judges and cops were in the pockets of organized crime, and you had just as much chance of taking a bullet from a cop as from a street thug. The streets were alive with the cacophony of wailing sirens, gunfire, and bloody screams of anguish.

Throughout all this chaos and anarchy, I was scraping to make a living in a post-punk rock and roll world where nobody knew exactly what they were fighting for. Was it the Iranians that Carter warned us about or protecting ourselves against the addicts and pushers out on the street? Of being a step or two ahead of another coked-up junkie looking to bury a shiv in your ribs? The high society safely tucked away in their fancy Manchester towers never really knew what life was like down here between the garbage bins and discarded needles littering the streets of Brooklyn. We were the inconvenient scum they chose to forget as they rushed past to another gala charity event. But what did I know? All of eighteen years old, the daughter of a strung-out mother that didn't know where she was half of the time and a father that disappeared when I was eight, never to return. I was the child of The Cure, Simple Minds, and The Ramones, spending most of my nights in smoke-filled places like the Mudd Club and Max's Kansas City, disappearing into the miasma and trying to forget about a world that didn't give a damn about us.

With the music came the drugs. I was a habitual user by the time I was thirteen, the rush of morphine and heroin my escape from the nightmares haunting my screwed-up life. So there I was again, crashing on another dirty sofa in an apartment God knows where in the city. Not even sure how I got here, just the beautiful release of a needle entering my vein again.

Pulling my fishnet stockings and leather bra straight again, I pushed some junkie's arm off me. He had fallen asleep next to me, though I couldn't remember where we met up. He was kinda cute though, in a scruffy sort of way. I dug around in my bag for my lipstick before scribbling my number on his forehead.

"Thanks for the rush, honey," I whispered, kissing him on the lips and heading for the door. Night had already fallen, and New York was humming with activity.

God, how long was I out for? I wondered, rubbing the needle marks on my arm. The prostitutes and pimps on the corners were doing brisk business as gangs of armed youths roamed around in packs, hollering at the moonlit sky. Anybody respectable with half a brain would be off the streets by the time the demons of the night came lurking about. Even the Mafioso in their shiny Lincoln Town Cars had the common sense to stay inside where it was safe. Like I said, New York back in '80 was a zoo, but I loved it. This was my world, and it accepted me for who I was— scum of the earth—and I was more than okay with that title.

A group of whores shouted a greeting at me from across the street before parading down to their next customer that pulled up to the curb. The johns would usually be high society types out looking for cheap fun; sometimes even a police squad car would show up. The ladies would often tell me about them when we sat drinking coffee before they went to work. We never tried to judge each other; we were all sucking on the fetid teat of New York City. And yet, they were some of the best and most courageous people I had ever met in my life. *I guess I should head on home.* It was not like Darla (my mother) would worry about me. She was most likely squirming under some fat bastard she picked up somewhere, too high to give much of a damn. But even for a street creature like me, midnight was a bad time to be around in the city.

"Taxi!" I waved down one of the grimy yellow-and-black vehicles. As it got closer, the driver saw me and sped up again, leaving me behind in his rearview mirrors, too afraid to pick up another strung-out junkie.

"Bitch!" I shouted, throwing an empty soda can after him. Guess I would be walking home tonight, already hearing Darla moaning and groaning at me in the morning. That is if she could find her way back to the apartment. It would not be the first time I went looking for her in the back rooms of cheap motels and abandoned subway stations.

You live a blessed life, Charlie. Sighing deeply, I headed home. Luckily, the weather was still semiwarm that time of year, and it made walking a breeze. It was about half an hour into my walk, just past the shuttered-up windows of Dellapietras butchery, when I heard the commotion. It sounded like a fight was brewing in the nearby back alley.

Walk away, this is not your fight. I had never really listened to my inner voice of warning and peered around the corner. A group of Nomads had cornered a man and was beating the living hell out of him. Their shouts raged, calling upon whatever god these street greasers prayed to while the man writhed in pain on the ground. I saw something glinting by the light of a nearby dustbin fire and walked closer. What made me do it, I'll never know, but for some strange reason my hands were calm as I picked up the Colt M1911A1, feeling the polished grip on my fingertips. The five gang members stopped and stared at me as I cocked the pistol over. They could not believe what they were seeing; a skimpily dressed teenager with dreadlocked red hair had the balls to be pointing a gun at them.

"What do you want, little girl?" the leader said, flicking open a switchblade and running it across his eyes. "Don't you know it's past your bedtime?" The rest of his gang snorted with laughter but soon grew quiet when they saw I wasn't moving. The leader's eyes narrowed in anger at my audacity, hands gripping tightly around a Louisville slugger.

"Cut the bitch!" the Nomads yelled in unison and ran down the alley toward me. Everything became quiet around me: the shouting of the gang members, the whine of a nearby air conditioner, even the sounds of cars rushing past. There was nothing but the steady rhythmic beating of my heart and my shallow breathing. The gun moved as if it was part of me, an organic extension of my body, firing four shots in a heartbeat. Ghosting between flailing fists and razor-sharp knives like they never existed, I sensed the bodies falling around me, almost in slow motion, as they hit the ground. My luck finally ran out as I spun around, a knife piercing deep into my stomach. Falling backwards against the alleyway, bright red blood flowing from the wound, I keeled over in pain. Rapidly fading in and out of consciousness, I saw the last remaining gang member standing over me, switchblade in hand. Before he could finish me off, his eyes rolled back in his head and he slumped forward. The man I saw earlier was standing over him, bloody baseball bat in hand. He gingerly lifted me up in his arms and carried me past the bodies as I clung tightly to his shoulder.

The last thing I remember before passing out was his gruff but reassuring words: "Shh, shh *passerotto*, I got you. I got you."

"*Calmati, Calmati . . .*"

CHAPTER FOUR

I'll never forget the night when they dragged me into that operating room, semiconscious with blood streaming from the wound in my stomach. There was chaos around me, doctors screaming for bandages and scalpels while nurses frantically ran around. I remember them lifting me up on the operating table and placing a chloroformed rag over my face as I struggled mightily to get free.

Why didn't it take? Why am I still awake? The thoughts flashed through my mind, interspersed between red flashes of absolute pain. Was I meant to experience all this? To feel every second of harrowing pain? Perhaps my punishment for killing those four men last night was that the universe had turned its back on me. I didn't want to; they came at me and I had no choice but to shoot them.

My back arched in agony, my eyes rolling white as the scalpel cut into me.

"Hold her down, dammit!" Five pairs of hands clung on grimly while the surgeon sliced through damaged sinews and torn flesh, sweat dripping down his blood-soaked vest. I could see the light in front of me, shining impossibly bright. Was it the light of heaven or the distant fires of hell? I was so close now, reaching out, fingers twitching in anticipation of the sweet release. All the pain, all the suffering from my dammed existence would be gone in an instant, nothing left to fight for, nothing at all.

"Let me go, let me go," I murmured incoherently to the sound of a heart monitor beeping behind me. All became quiet, and the dirty room and all the people faded from view, replaced with the blissful sight of pure darkness. Did I smile in those last few moments? Was it laughter at the looks of horror on the surgeon's and nurses' faces? That this damned child was still alive somehow? Who the hell cared? I was finally free.

Sunlight. Warm, nurturing, embracing. I felt its warm rays on my face, soothing my tired body.

Blinking at the sudden light, I tried to sit up but instantly regretted it. The pain from my stomach shot through my body and I lay back, gasping for air.

Where am I? It looked like some sort of apartment; I could hear the sounds of the city outside, of cars and ambulances rushing past in the distance. It was a grimy and barely kept up sort of place, nothing I wasn't used to. I saw a man sitting by a rickety wooden table in the corner, reading a newspaper as smoke drifted from a cigarette in his mouth. He finally looked up and raised an eyebrow in my direction.

"Glad to see you're finally awake. Welcome back, kid." He was of medium build, maybe late thirties, and not muscular, but he clearly took care of himself.

Dressed in elegant pants with a white vest, his hair was black and slicked back with slightly too much Brylcreem. I had a habit of noticing little details and watched with detached interest as he folded an olive-skinned hand over a cup of still hot coffee.

"Who are you? What is this place?" I asked, still confused at how exactly I got here.

"You can call me Vince, and we brought you here to keep you safe. You survived by the skin of your teeth, and I didn't think you would make it." He flashed me a slightly ironic smile before turning his attention to the newspaper.

"You can't keep me here. I want to go home." Clutching my side and feeling the coarse bandages under my fingers, I tried to get up from the bed. I barely made it two steps to the door when I heard him chuckling to himself.

"And go where exactly? You got no idea what's going on out there, do you? Sit down and I'll tell you." He downed his coffee as I reluctantly sat back down on the bed, never taking my eyes off him.

"Talk." I was not in the mood for long discussions, and I still felt like I had been run over by a train.

"You started a shitstorm last night when you shot those four Nomads. As we speak, they are tearing up Brooklyn looking for you. A gang hit is one thing, but to lose four members in one night and to a girl of all people? It's a massive humiliation and hit to their reputation, and they want your blood at all costs."

"I didn't want to shoot them. They came at me and I had no choice." Turning my head and looking out the window, I didn't want to look him in the eyes.

"That doesn't matter. I would not give much for your chances if they catch you out on the street. And when they are finished with you, they will go after your parents and anyone you ever loved."

I ignored the comment about my parents and looked at him over my shoulder. "So what do we do now?"

Vincent paused for a moment and thought it through, sseeming to roll the thought around in his head

. "You sit tight till tonight at least, then I'm moving you out of Brooklyn and down to the West Village. I know a couple of queers down there who owe me a favor. They will keep you safe till things quiet down again. You will fit in nicely with that bunch of freaks."

"I see." Chewing my fingernails, I looked him deep in the eyes. "Why were those men beating you up?" Part of me knew the answer, but I wanted to hear him say it.

"I enforce outstanding loans for the Gambino family, and I was just finishing up last night when those five punks jumped me. They were trying to strong-arm me when you arrived. Damn good timing on your part I must say."

I shook my head and pinched my nose. My life had come down between two choices: stay here with a Mafia thug or take my chances with the gangs outside.

"You don't approve of my lifestyle choices?" Vince said with a slight smirk on his face.

"I don't know what to think anymore." I stopped for a moment, unsure if I should ask the question. "Why did you save me? You could have easily left me there to die."

He ran his hand through his hair, straightening it back

perfectly before speaking. "Something made me do it. You are most likely more trouble than you are worth, but I couldn't just leave you to those animals.

"Tell me something." He smacked his lips a few times before continuing. "Which gang do you belong to? I know most of the associates in the five families and you are not one of them, so you must be gang affiliated to be trained so well."

"Not in a gang, and I never fired a weapon before in my life," I replied calmly.

"Bullshit. You mean to tell me some punk kid is able to take down four gang members in the time it takes to spit and she has never so much as touched a gun before?" he exclaimed in Italian.

"Believe what you want to." I really didn't care if he bought my story or not. It didn't matter to me.

"*Incredibile*," he muttered to himself, throwing on his shirt and pulling on a brown leather jacket. "There're some clean clothes, and I left you a few sandwiches in the fridge. I have to clock in and make some preparations for your arrival. Make sure you are ready to leave by tonight. We can't risk you staying any longer in Brooklyn than is necessary." He headed for the door, then stopped and turned back to me. "And thanks for saving my ass back there, kid. I appreciate it."

I was left alone again with my thoughts as I slowly lifted myself off the bed and opened a nearby drawer. Looking back in disgust at the door and mentally cursing Vince, I held up a long, flowery dress and blouse. Where he found it was beyond me, but I had no choice; my old clothes were blood stained and ruined.

With great pain, I finally got dressed and grabbed a seat by the table. The sandwiches were at least a day old but they tasted heavenly as I slathered tomato sauce on the bologna. Sitting back after I had eaten, I took stock of my situation.

You can walk out of that door right now, but then what? Constantly looking over your shoulder till some thug cuts your throat? And what about Darla? She might be an uncaring bitch, but she's still your mother and you can't let anything happen to her. The only option I had was to play along with the Mafioso's game till I could figure out what he wanted. How could my life get screwed up so quickly? It wasn't perfect, but at least it was better than being carted around goddamn New York by the Mafia. Lying back on the bed, I closed my eyes and sighed deeply.

What a life, Charlie, what a life.

Just after six that evening, I heard a knocking on the door. Vince was back.

"Quickly now, we have to go." He didn't say much further, handing me a long overcoat and rushing me down the eerily quiet corridor of the apartment building. A town car and driver were already waiting for us, the engine humming impatiently. Looking up and down the street, Vince pushed me into the car and nodded at the driver. The Lincoln smoothly set off, and I could see Brooklyn's buildings sweep past us. The demons of the night, the fanatics and freaks that owned the street were slowly emerging from their slumber.

For them, life carried on as usual, and they took no notice of the child being swept away to God knows where. We even saw a group of Nomads hunkered down in an alleyway. They were clearly gearing up for war as I slunk down in the soft leather seats despite the darkly tinted windows. Why did I have this strange feeling that I was leaving my old life behind and that the unknown was waiting for me?

Twenty-five-odd minutes later, we stopped at a nondescript brownstone building in the West Village. The streets were relatively quiet, with only a few stragglers out as Vince hurried me out of the car toward a locked hair salon. I raised an eyebrow in his direction but said nothing.

"Trust me. Now listen carefully and you remember your manners, okay? These fruits may be strange, but they are family. They'll take good care of you till I can figure something out." He rang the doorbell as I looked at him with a grin on my face.

"Family?" I asked.

"You shut up. It's my sister-in-law's brother and his partner." Before he could say anything further, a short, stubby man with blond, spiky hair stuck his head out of the door and examined us up and down. "Peter, sweetie, you had better come look what the cat's dragged in," he called back into the shop before addressing me. "Oh, honey, you didn't spend too much time with this animal did you? And what in the good Lord's name are you wearing?" He looked up at Vince with a mock accusing look before kissing him on the cheek.

"Vincenzo, is this the girl you were talking about? Well, don't just stand there like a drag queen waiting for a lay. Come on in."

"This is my brother-in-law Richard, or is it Susan today? I can never tell," Vincent said, introducing me to the loudly dressed man. "I can't stay, and I need to get back to Brooklyn tonight. You okay with taking care of her for a few days?"

"Do you even have to ask? Now shoo, you are making the place look untidy." The odd man ushered me inside as Vince returned back to the car, where it quickly disappeared down the road a few minutes later.

Oh, Charlie, what have you gotten yourself into? I wondered to myself as the salon door slammed shut behind me.

CHAPTER FIVE

The late afternoon sun had just disappeared behind the nearby skyscrapers and the room was tinted in the faintly yellow glow of the Village streetlights. I could smell the faint leftover fragrance of shampoo and hair care products in the salon as I looked over the now quiet row of hair dryers standing idly by. It was an eclectic but elegant sort of place, and I could just see women of all ages chatting away in the chairs while stylists scurried around them. For a moment, I stopped and stared back at the now closed door behind me.

Maybe it would be better just to go out there and take my chances on the street, I thought glumly to myself, already worried what would happen to me if the Nomads found me. "Come along, dear," said the man in the red smoking jacket, taking me by the arm and leading me up a flight of stairs to an apartment above. "Peter? Did you hear me?"

"I heard you, dahling," a voice responded from the top of the stairs. "Just got some biscuits in the oven. Be with you now."

"Oh, God. Just say nothing, okay?" Richard muttered to me, rolling his eyes heavenward as if to look for some sort of spiritual intervention. I said nothing and raised an eyebrow in his direction. I didn't want to admit it, but I was ravenous with hunger, the paltry sandwiches of earlier long forgotten as we headed up the stairs.

The kitchen was beautiful and inviting, painted a deep, dark red with fairy lights hanging from the ceiling. A slightly middle-aged man, thin as a reed with dyed black hair, was just pulling out a tray from the oven and putting it down on the counter. He turned around and looked at me in horror.

"Oh, honey, who did that to you? What is that? Hippie chic meets Honolulu? That dress can turn a gay man straight. Richard, why is this fashion faux pas in my kitchen?" His voice was high and effeminate, but there was a warmth and sense of kindness about him. I liked Peter instantly.

"Peter, this is the girl that Vincent mentioned earlier, remember? He wants us to take care of . . ." Richard paused and tapped his fingers on his belly. "Do we have a name, dahling?" he asked as a slight smile formed on his face.

"Charlie. My mother calls me Charlotte, but I don't like that name. I don't want to be an inconvenience, and I can go if you don't want me here."

"I do love the name Charlotte; she sounds like royalty. I used that stage name many years ago. We like this one already. She has spunk about her. Now sit and I'll get you something to eat while Richard fetches one of my old dresses. One that is less likely to give Stevie Wonder a stroke."

"We will just have to take it in a bit on the hips," Richard said matter-of-factly before quickly disappearing down the hall.

"I heard that!" shouted Peter with a glint in his eye, reaching behind him and placing a steaming-hot biscuit in front of me. "Just ignore him, dear. He has been bitchy since I told him his solo rendition of *La Carlotta* was overdone and pitchy. Now eat. Enjoy!" He busied himself happily cleaning the kitchen while I took a bite of the pastry. Stopping and chewing slower and slower, I looked up at Peter with a worried look and tapped the biscuit a few times on the edge of the table. It clunked heavily, but I didn't want to say anything, seeing as he was so nice to me. Carefully, I hid the hard, possible future homicide weapon in my jacket pocket, hearing Richard coming down the hall again.

"If you picked that ghastly yellow sunflower dress from the back of my closet again, I swear to the good Lord I will put rat poison in your coffee," Peter said without looking back.

"Calm your tits, dahling, I found something just perfect for her." It was a narrow black and blue dress, and I had to admit it looked amazing. "It was one of Peter's about sixty pounds and ten meltdowns ago. Now, go put it on and we can talk a bit."

He eyed the plate of biscuits and looked up at me, saying nothing, but I could see the sympathy in his eyes as he showed me down the hall. It was weird being welcomed so warmly by people I barely knew, and I wasn't sure what to make of it.

Don't get used to it, Charlie. I knew there would come a time when I had to run again, and I didn't want to get too comfortable. Trouble would always come looking for me; it was just a fact of my life. When I returned from changing about twenty minutes later, Richard and Peter were sitting by the dining room table, waiting for me.

"Brava! Brava!" they cheered, and poured another cup of coffee. "Now you are starting to look like something, and we can sort out the hairdo later. This ain't Jamaica, dear. The Rasta locks have to go." Richard took a sip of coffee and looked at me intently. "Now tell us about you and don't leave out any details. Vincent told us you were in trouble, but he didn't mention any particulars. We are all ears."

I sighed deeply, drumming my fingers on the coffee cup before speaking, telling them about the incident in the alley and how I shot the four Nomads. Of how Vincent carried me to safety and how the surgeons managed to save my life.

"I didn't want to kill them." My eyes shot full of tears. "It happened so quickly. What am I supposed to do now? They won't give up till I'm dead, and I don't know what to do." Shaking my head, I looked out of the second-story window to the firefly lights of the city outside. "Honey," Peter said calmly, holding my hand in his. "We both know what it is to live in fear, not knowing which asshole with a hard-on for bashing gays around is coming for us next. But we cannot let those bastards get the better of us, and we must approach each day, each performance, with our chins lifted high."

Richard gently kissed him on the cheek. "I have never loved you more. Now Charlie, you will be safe here and we will take of you, but it's your choice, dear. There are a lot of strange and very nasty people out there, and it's no place for a young girl to be about. What do you say, dahling?"

Biting my lip, I nodded in the affirmative, smiling when they clapped their hands together and hugged me tightly.

"Oh, mahvellous! Just mahvellous!" Richard continued, "And you can have all the biscuits you want." We laughed heartily at the inside joke as Peter looked at us, mystified. When the laughter died away, something came to me. A question I had on my mind earlier that was bugging me.

"What did Vince mean when he said he often did business with you? What aren't you telling me?"

Peter and Richard looked at each other, talking in a body language that only couples who have been together for years have.

"Do we?"

"We could . . ."

"But what if she tells someone?"

"Vincent vouched for her . . ."

"Vince is an animal."

"I'd love to get my claws into him. Rhoar."

"At your age, you'd have to get a hip replacement."

"If I'm lucky."

"Guys!" I interrupted them. "What are you not telling me?"

They stopped their discussion and looked at me.

Finally, Peter spoke and I could see the worry in his eyes. "You must understand, dahling, that if this gets out to the wrong ears, our lives will not be worth a penny."

"Exactly," replied Richard. "This is life and death we are talking about here. Well, I guess Vincent will tell you eventually, so we might as well show you."

"Show me what, exactly?" They were hiding something, and my patience was growing thin.

"Well, you see, the salon is just one of the businesses we run. We also provide stage props to all the local theatres here in the city, and it's actually the perfect cover." Richard sighed and rose from his chair. "Come along, it's best we show you." We headed down the stairs to the basement underneath the building.

Peter pulled away a couple of boxes and placed his hand on an iron ring in the floor. "If you tell anyone, we are going to pull your fingernails out personally."

I nodded and watched as he pulled back the ring. As he reached down and flipped on a light switch, I could see there was a hole in the floor. "After you, young lady," he said, and stepped back as I cautiously moved down the rickety wooden steps. It took me a moment to realize what I was staring at; it was a fantastic sight to see, beyond anything I had ever imagined.

"What the hell guys? What the hell?" I kept repeating over and over again.

It was just not possible. Just not possible.

CHAPTER SIX

I still couldn't believe my eyes as I looked back at Richard and Peter. They smiled sheepishly at me, like two naughty schoolboys that had been caught in the act. Slowly, I walked down the remainder of wooden steps to the brightly lit basement underneath me.

Guns. The entire room from floor to ceiling was packed with a mind-blowing assortment of weaponry and ammunition. From simple pistols to shotguns, gleaming semiautomatics and even a sniper rifle lay silently waiting for me. I even glanced at boxes of land mines and grenades in the corner, all with military seals on them. Running my hand through a crate of ammunition and feeling the metal-coated rounds under my fingers, I looked back up the steps at the two figures behind me.

"Guys? Care to explain?" I asked, more curious than angry at them. Do not ask me why, but it was the very last thing I expected of them. They seemed so innocent and harmless. Richard pulled his red smoking jacket straight and walked over to me, placing his hand on my shoulder.

"You see, sweetie, times are tough, and there is not much money to be made in the hairdressing gig. And seeing as we both were in the military before they kicked us out—"

"For being way too delicious for them," interrupted Peter casually, cleaning his nails.

"That we were, dear. So we kept some of our military contacts, and you know how army supplies tend to just disappear. Well, we took advantage of that situation to start our own little mom-and-pop shop."

"Just with a massive lot of weapons and ammunition?" I replied, trying my best to hide a smile.

"Oh, pish pash. It's just a technicality, dahling. Some people sell cream cakes; we sell guns and bullets. They'll both kill you eventually, so what's the difference?" Richard stated matter-of-factly, running a cleaning cloth over a line of AK47s.

"I see. And where does the theatre stage prop part come into it?"

"Our simple but brilliant disguise. Darling Peter thought of it. We supply stage props to all the local theatres and movie production companies in the city, but in between, we move the real guns to those silly souls who feel like killing themselves. The delightful people at the NYPD have no idea what we are doing right under their noses."

"And you are not worried about what those guns are doing to the city?" I asked curiously.

"It's a war zone out there, and those animals will always find ways to off themselves, be it with knives or our guns. In our defense, we only supply weapons to the mob. Say what you want about them, but there is a code of honor about them, not like those filthy street gangs," Peter said, trying to look away from me, but I could see the shame in his eyes.

"They threw a brick through our shop window last week and spray-painted our front door. It took us hours to scrub it off. I know you might not agree with what we're doing, but we're just trying to make a living here." Richard hugged a downcast Peter tightly around the shoulders.

It took me a moment, but I looked them straight in the eyes. "I understand. Since my father left us behind, I had to scrape for everything in life. And Mom? They only thing she is interested in is where her next high is coming from. So I guess you got to do what you got to do. I just never expected it from you two."

"Nobody ever suspects the fags, dear," Richard said, laughing loudly as he hugged us both tightly. It felt strange, being so readily accepted by people I had only just met. I wanted to run, but I heard my inner voice rise above my doubts.

Stay, Charlie, you will be safe here.

When everything quieted down again, Peter crossed his arms and appeared to think deeply about something. We both jumped as he suddenly and loudly proclaimed, "We must go out tonight! The girls will want to meet Charlie, and I am in no mood to sit around here all night. What do you say?"

"Sounds good. We can even take them some of your biscuits," Richard mumbled with just a slight touch of acid in his voice.

"What's that, dear?"

"Nothing. But we cannot take Charlie out like this. You go find her something fabulous to wear while I do her hair. We cannot be seen with someone that looks like a Jamaican refugee washed up in New York Harbor. Onwards, my dear Peter. There is much to do!"

Richard was a blur of movement as he shooed us both out. I stopped for a moment, watching him head up the wooden steps.

"Don't I have any say in this? Vincent said I should lay low for a bit."

Richard took me firmly but gently by the arm and walked me out. "No, dahling, you have no say in this matter, and dearest Vincent can go blow a duck for all I care. We shall be the belles of the ball tonight! Forwards!"

I tried to hide my smile but failed miserably as the wonderful man took me back up to the salon, locking the trapdoor behind him and pulling the wooden box back over it.

The next hour and a bit was probably the happiest time I had ever experienced in my life. Richard was a blur of hands while he untied my dreadlocks and started washing my hair, constantly talking about his life in the army and how he met Peter before being kicked out of the armed services for being homosexual. Of how he found happiness and started the salon in the Village. All the while, Peter rushed in and out with an assortment of dresses, each one casually dismissed with a shake of the head or a catty comment from Richard.

"Do you want her to hate herself?"

"This is not New Jersey, dahling."

"Is that from the Ray Charles collection?"

And on and on. I looked on with amazement as he started cutting my hair, long red locks falling to the floor, like a part of me was being left behind. He turned me away from the mirror as he started coloring my hair. Finally, Peter arrived with an elegant and slim black dress, and Richard nodded his approval.

"Go get dressed, honey. We will wait for you. Oh, and there are some shoes in the dresser as well." They looked on, smiling, as I disappeared from the room.

What are you doing, Charlie? This is not your place, I kept thinking to myself as I slipped the dress over my shoulders and reached for the shoes.

I'm busy living. Taking a deep breath and walking down the steps, I saw Richard and Peter waiting for me. They were already dressed in their outfits and broke into massive smiles when they saw me.

"How do I look?" I asked, feeling very self-conscious suddenly. But I needn't have worried, as they hugged me tightly.

"Perfect, honey. Just perfect. Oh, you are going to knock them dead!" Laughing and smiling, the two locked arms with me and we walked out of the salon.

"Taxi!" shouted Peter as we waited for the yellow cab to pull up before pilling in. While I watched the people and the buildings of New York flash past me, I thought how strange and amazing life was. Only a day ago, I was just another street urchin looking for the next party and the next high, and now I had met these two wonderful men who happened to be arms dealers of all things, and they had accepted me as one of their own, without judgment or prejudice. And now I was in a beautiful dress and going God knows where and . . . It was crazy, and just a bit much to take in. I slumped down in the faded middle seat of the New York cab, the voices and chattering fading away around me.

You know this cannot last, Charlie. Good things just don't happen to you. Somewhere out there in the dark expanses of the city, the Nomads are looking for your blood. And then there is the Mafia as well. Heaven knows what they want with you. This cannot last, Charlie; you know it.

But I didn't want to accept it. I wanted to be happy and free and live my life like I wanted to. No more looking over my shoulder, no more fear. To leave the old Charlie behind and never look back. To be the girl with the short black hair in her beautiful dress, surrounded by the two most wonderful scoundrels in the world. That wasn't asking too much, was it?

Just a content and happy life. That's all I wanted.

Nothing more.

I snuggled safely into Richard's shoulder, the million firefly lights of the city dancing in my eyes as we headed into the night. The world could pass me by and I couldn't have cared less. This was where I belonged, and this was where I was happy.

Right here.

CHAPTER SEVEN

It was surreal, watching the people on the streets as we passed them by. They danced like there was no tomorrow—no wars, no Ayatollah Khomeini, no Carter, just nothing but the music and the beat. Through the open cab window, I could hear their singing and laughter on the evening wind, and it was beautiful. It was free and magical to my ears. Maybe it was the forgotten hippies left behind at Woodstock that missed the bus to Nirvana, trying to forget the screwed-up world they lived in.

I wished for a moment that I could also forget, but I knew my demons would always be a step behind me. It would always be my reality.

"Where are we going?" I asked Peter, seeing him staring deep in thought out of the window.

"The Limelight. It's an old church on Seventh Avenue that they converted into a dance club. You'll like it there, I know. The music is great, and the people are fantastic."

"Could you ever imagine two queers like us ever being allowed in there a couple of years ago? They would have had a fucking heart attack," Richard replied dryly as I heard Peter snort in laughter next to me. I couldn't help but smile as they roared with laughter, tears rolling down their cheeks. They tried saving their mascara from being ruined, but it was too late, and none of us really cared. With the fits of laughter slowly dying away, the cab driver calmly turned down onto Seventh Avenue, and there I saw it.

The old church was still gorgeous with its tiled roofs and stained glass windows. I never cared much for church, and it was never my scene, to be honest, but something about the black-stoned building struck me , something spiritual and unexplainable. Even from down the street, I could hear the music and the people hanging around outside. Dressed in all the colors of the rainbow with the wildest and biggest hair imaginable, they seemed like visitors from another world to me. I was a long way from the grungy cesspools where I usually hung out, but strangely enough, it didn't matter to me.

"Now remember that you are eighteen, dear, and don't worry about the bouncers; they know us. And Peter, sweetie, please do not flirt with the hired muscle at the door again, okay? You nearly got us killed last time around."

"I was this close to landing that hottie that usually works Tuesday nights. This close." Peter sighed happily and straightened his long blond wig.

"I remember two forty-something drag queens running like mad down the streets of the Village with a three-hundred-pound gorilla behind them after you tried to kiss him. But anyhoo, let's own this thing, girls!" he proclaimed, linking arms with us and marching determinedly to the club's entrance. The place was wild and jumping, and music thundered through every inch of the room. I felt alive, like pure energy was pumping through my veins as the smoke-filled space embraced us. The bouncers only nodded at us, and I saw Richard calmly but firmly drag a dreamy-eyed Peter away from the block of muscle at the door.

"Come along, dear. They should already be here. Where are they? Over there! Yoohoo!" Richard shouted, waving his arms madly. I barely had time to catch my breath or stare at the wonderfully eclectic people around me when I was seized by the arm and dragged across the dance floor to a private booth at the far end of the club. It was the weirdest and strangest looking group of people I had ever seen, sitting by themselves and downing glass after glass of cheap champagne. I couldn't help but stare at their wonderfully over-the-top wigs, long sparkly dresses, and overdone makeup as they hugged Peter and Richard tightly. Suddenly, I felt very self-conscious, like I didn't belong, but there was no time for protest as the drag queens rushed me and embraced me like an old friend.

"Girls, this is Charlie, and she is staying with us for a little bit. Charlie, this is the finest and most drunkest bunch of ladies you will ever meet. We are all the dropouts and lost souls of society, queens of the night one and all." I could see the warmth and love in Peter's eyes as he talked about his friends.

"Where did you all meet?" I asked as they poured me a glass of champagne. I had never tasted it before, but I instantly liked it.

"Some are army dropouts, tired of that wrinkly old man in the White House's bullshit. Some we met doing the theatre scene in the seventies. Others we met along the way, and we've been friends ever since. Raise your glasses, bitches, to Charlie, and we are damn glad to have her here. Cheers!"

There was laughter and singing galore as we toasted. For once, I didn't feel like a freak and a washout, like I could be myself here without anyone judging me. I had the most marvelous of times as we danced the night away, and I even got to slow dance with a burly Black man in stilettos and a very tight silver dress who called herself Amanda.

There was nothing sexual or weird about it, just friends dancing and trying to forget the world and its misery outside. I won't lie and say there weren't any drugs involved; I was offered lines of cocaine, but something in me compelled me to pass on it. I wanted to bury the messed-up junkie inside me always looking for the next high, and besides, I wanted to enjoy the moment and the people around me. Maybe I was a fool or deluded to think I could just wish my old life away, but for those magical few hours in that smoky club in the Village, surrounded by the most interesting and magnificent people imaginable, I wanted to believe I could be free again.

By two o'clock, we started saying our goodbyes, hugging each other and promising to stay in touch as the music started to fade away. All the fabulous people of the night were heading off home or wherever to sleep away the next morning's hangovers.

As we left the club behind, walking slowly down the now quiet streets of the Village and looking for a cab, I felt Richard tug my arm.

"Well, dear? Did you enjoy it? It wasn't too weird for you,

was it?" he asked with a worried frown on his face.

"No," I replied. "It was perfect. I have never known much happiness in my life, but somehow everything just felt right in there, like the world could just pass me by and I wouldn't care even one little bit."

"Good, I'm glad you enjoyed—" He was suddenly interrupted as we heard the shrill sounds of whistling behind us. Three men carrying knives and clubs had emerged from the alley behind us.

"Hey, look at the goddamn faggots, walking on our streets like they own them!" one ratlike figure shouted to his friends, eliciting a loud series of jeers and laughter.

"Just ignore them," Richard said, pulling me by the sleeve. "Just a bunch of drunk bullies looking for kicks. Come on, and we'll find a taxi to take us home."

"What's the matter, fags? Why you ignoring us?" They kept coming after us, whistling and shouting. It was like time stopped and everything around me grew quiet. I could sense the brick as it left the man's hand, feel the texture of the rough red grain as it flew through the air. In slow motion, I pushed Peter to the side, feeling him fall away as I turned and felt the brick strike my chest. Chest thumping, blood dripping down my breasts, dress torn as I lay on the dirty pavement sucking in deep swathes of breath. I could not hear Richard's terrified screams or the laughter of the men, just the torrent of blood in my veins racing faster and faster.

And then it stopped.

Slowly, I got to my feet, face emotionless and deadly calm. The hate was palpable in the man's eyes as he swung for my head. I never moved, hand reaching out, catching the club in mid-swing; disarming him in one move and driving the steel club into his throat.

He fell backwards, clutching a crushed larynx while I moved like a wraith behind the second man, catching his neck in a vice-like grip and slamming it backwards, bones splintering in a horrific concerto. The last man, the rat-like one, barely had time to think, dropping his switchblade and running for his life. With deadly precision, I picked up the knife and threw it, hitting him squarely in the back. He lay squirming as I walked slowly over to him, pulling the knife out and cutting his tendons one by one.

And then I hit him.

Over and over again, till the blood pooled sickly red and my knuckles were worn down to the bone. I was a woman apart, cut off from myself and everything around me. My only goal was to destroy this man till there was nothing left of him. I only stopped when I felt Peter and Richard pull me off him. The world shifted back into focus and there I was: alone on the streets of New York City, just a girl in a torn dress with blood and tears running down her face. I slowly got up and walked way, feeling a hand on my shoulder.

"Charlie . . ." Richard wanted to say something, but I pushed him away.

"Leave me alone. For God's sake, leave me alone. Look at me. I don't know who I am. I don't know who I am." Holding up my bloody hands, I started to shake uncontrollably, tears streaming down my face. To my amazement, Peter and Richard hugged me tightly.

"We got you, dearie, we got you" was all I could hear through the ragged tears as I held on to them with everything I had in me.

"Who am I? Who am I?" I kept repeating to myself as they led me away, head hanging low and a coat wrapped warmly around my shoulders. I left three broken bodies behind me, their blood dripping down and away into the sewers. The police would later classify it simply as a gangland attack, but all around the Village, it came to be known as the Seventh Avenue massacre. The trannies and the addicts that walked the night told the tale of the demon in a dress, and her bloody story that started that one fateful night as she and her companions came from the club, how she butchered three men in the space of a heartbeat without even blinking. Some said it was the cruel act of a murderous animal, others that she simply protected those she loved and cherished. However it may seem, the Village was about to be set on fire, and she was right there in the middle of it. There on the lonely streets of the West Village, between the discarded needles and rubbish bags, the strange and blood-drenched legend of Charlotte Corday started.

And how she brought hell itself to New York City.

CHAPTER EIGHT

Last night was a blur, the ragged images flashing past me like reels off an old movie projector. All I could remember was Richard and Peter walking me home and putting me in the shower when we got back, my bloody clothes laying in a still pile as the warm water ran across my shivering skin, mixing with the tears running down my cheeks. I tried washing the blood off my hands, scrubbing till there was no skin left, but it was to no avail. It would not come out, no matter how hard I tried. The faces of the men I murdered, I saw their final moments as they stared at me in horror before I ended their lives. Did they have names or family they cared for? Did it matter who they were?

It was you or them, Charlie; if you hadn't acted when you did, you would all be dead now. You had no choice, Charlie. You had no choice. I absolutely hated the feeling of helplessness that swirled around me. How dare they force me into this corner, into this decision, when I wanted nothing to do with it? My life was far from perfect, but it was still mine, and I controlled it, not them.

Whoever that person was who took over my body for those few blood-soaked moments, I want her gone and I want her dead! I slammed my fist into the cream-colored shower tiles, shattering one and instantly feeling bad about it. Peter and Richard had been nothing but kind to me, and I had no right to wreck their place. Bless their massive hearts, anyone else would have most likely left me back there on the streets and never looked back. But there they were, waiting with a big, warm jersey and a bowl of hot soup for me when I got out of the shower.

They said nothing, just smiling and milling around the kitchen happily. I thought it strange why anyone would be this warm and forgiving to someone they barely knew. Running a finger through the rapidly cooling minestrone soup, I wanted to say something but bit my lip, thinking it would be better to remain quiet.

"You're wondering why we haven't thrown you out yet, right?" Peter said, packing away dishes without looking back at me.

"Well, kinda, yeah. I can't figure it out."

"It's simple, dear. We both know what it feels like to be outcasts and unsure of who you really are. Peter and I had our demons growing up in this wretched city and going through the army, but we embraced our inner true selves. Once you do that, they cannot hurt you again," replied Richard, smiling and tapping me gently on my hand.

"But I don't know who I am." I pushed the bowl away and sighed deeply, looking past the yellow curtained window.

"We'll help you with that, dahling. You just got to stick with us; we'll be your fairy godmothers so long as you need us. Now, it's bedtime, young lady. You've had a long and very busy day.

When you wake up in the morning, I'll have some fresh biscuits waiting for you. Off you go now."

"You'll do more damage with those blasted biscuits than the child ever did," grumbled Richard under his breath, just loud enough for me to hear.

"What's that, dear?"

"Nothing, nothing at all. Come along, Charlie. I'll make up the spare bedroom for you." We quickly disappeared before Peter could say anything further.

The room was just right, and I soon settled in for the night. Finally, the apartment became quiet a few minutes later, but there was still too much on my mind for me to fall asleep just yet. I heard the sounds of the city outside, the police sirens hunting through the nighttime caverns of the steel and iron jungle.

Are they looking for me? I wondered, laying my head back on the goose feather pillow. I thought back to the club and the wonderful people I met there, the look on the man's face as I beat him to death with my bare hands, and finally I thought of Peter and Richard—the most marvelously weird people I had ever met in my life.

"Thanks, guys" I whispered softly before falling asleep as the night finally claimed me.

The next two weeks were a strange time to be around in the Village. Everyone was on edge after news of the Seventh Avenue massacre became public. Even the street grease that owned the night were wary to come out alone when the sun went down. They would often speak of the demon in hushed tones and how she just disappeared into thin air after that night's events. I heard through the grapevine that the police had looked into it before passing it off to the Feds. New York's finest didn't really care about the denizens of the Village. We were all just freaks to them, best out of the way and forgotten as soon as possible.

Peter and Richard gave me a job as an assistant in the hair salon downstairs, sweeping up hair and answering the phone. It was perfect, and I felt it best to stay as far away as possible from the gun smuggling side of the business. I was content and happy for once.

Life had just started to get back to normal when he walked in. It was shortly after lunchtime on that Monday afternoon, and we were just finishing up with a client when I heard the door swinging open. A chill down my spine made me hold back, slinking behind the storeroom curtain as I peered out. He was mid-twenties, about six foot three, with a calm presence that some could easily mistake for being lackadaisical, but with deep green eyes that picked up every detail around him. A slight scar ran across his left hand and he subconsciously pulled a sleeve back over it. Folding a strand of well-kept blond hair behind his ear, he reached for a badge inside his long, black trench coat while Peter walked closer.

"My name is Agent Christopher Monroe, FBI, and I just want to ask a few questions if that is okay with you?" The voice was cold and calculated, every subtle nuance measured and quantified to an exact standard.

"Not at all if you don't mind me cleaning up a bit while we talk." Peter busied himself putting cans of hairspray away.

"Tell me, you and the other gentleman who resides in the apartment upstairs, you are frequent patrons of the local nightclubs in the West Village, yes?"

"We hang out there if that is what you mean. How did you know that?"

"We are the government, sir. It's our job to find out things, and the residents around here are always willing to talk with the right kind of motivation. Did you visit an establishment known as the Limelight on the twenty-third of this month?" He was careful not to overdo it, pulling ever so slightly on the strings, testing and probing along the way.

"We met some friends for drinks there. Is that a crime?"

"Not at all." He tapped a perfectly sharp pencil on a notepad before speaking further. "And did you happen to witness anything related to the unfortunate events that occurred on Seventh Avenue that evening?"

"I'm sorry, but no. We saw nothing that could help your investigation." The hesitation in Peter's voice was gone in a split second, but it was already too late. It was all the agent needed.

"Thank you for your time, and if you remember anything, here's my card." A razor-thin shard appeared in his elegant fingers and, without a word further, he turned and left, stopping only once to look behind him. Our eyes connected like two polar opposites fusing as one. What did he see in me? Guilt? Fear? Rage?

Whatever it was, I knew that our paths would cross again somewhere down the line. It would not be the last I saw of Agent Monroe. That was for damn sure.

The rest of the afternoon was quiet and without incident. The others didn't say much, but I could see the agent's visit had rattled them. Maybe it was the cache of assault weapons hidden in the basement, or perhaps he had just struck a nerve a little too close to home. Either way, I didn't mention it again.

We had just sat down for the evening supper, chicken cacciatore with mustard greens, when the doorbell rang. Thinking it suspicious that anyone would be calling that late, I excused myself and headed down the stairs. Slowly pulling the beadwork curtain back, I looked out on the street. Vincent was standing in front of the door, the orange streetlights casting a faint glow on his steely features. He had a look in his eye, the look of a man hell-bent on destruction. Blood, fire, and cyanide etched the corners of his eyes.

"Get your coat. We're starting tonight."

CHAPTER NINE

Vince said nothing further, turning and heading back to the still lingering car. He was evidently in a hurry, and something big was bothering him.

There's only trouble waiting for you if you go with him. Walk away, Charlie. Just walk away. I looked wistfully back to the darkened salon and the sounds of laughter coming from upstairs. A happy and content life was within my reach; just close the door and never look back. Then why was there a twisted and demented part of me that wanted to find out more? To walk the dark path and see where it led?

Do it. What do you have to lose? Go on, do it. Biting my lip and closing the door behind me, I slowly walked to the Town Car, its black paint tinged with swathes of nearby neon advertising signs. Vince looked around cautiously before climbing into the driver's seat. We set off down the slowly awakening streets, the street vendors wheeling their carts away. A local record store put on its lights, waiting for the night crowd to arrive, to drop by and listen to some killer beats while smoking the best and most wicked reefer around.

Vince's silence was getting to me as he pushed the car faster, weaving past yellow cabs and other Town Cars on his way.

"Are you going to tell me where we're going, or are we just going to sit here like a couple of idiots?" I asked, fiddling with the latch on the car's cubbyhole. Vince calmly but firmly put his hand on my mine and shook his head.

"Not here, just wait." He turned his attention back to the road, heading farther away from the Village. It was infuriating being kept in the dark, but I maintained my composure, trying not to let him see the anxiety building in me. Soon we had left the Bohemian city blocks behind, driving through the industrial area. It was quiet this late in the evening. A few workmen sat around on upturned crates, playing poker and puffing thin streams of tobacco smoke into the late afternoon air. They most likely didn't want to go home to their nagging wives and screaming children, I thought as Vince drove on. Wherever we were going, he knew exactly which route to take. I said nothing, just watching the world pass by. For all the talk of America being the best country in the world, it was a sight that we street demons knew well enough by now—the homeless lying under tattered strips of cardboard, the lost souls of the night beatboxing around iron drums filled with orange fire. Though I didn't know it at the time, this was the America our soon-to-be-elected president, Reagan, and the execs on Wall Street never wanted to see, the nightmare creeping gently into the backs of their minds, constantly there no matter how hard they tried to forget it.

Finally, I felt the car start to slow down. The smell of rotting fish hung vaporlike in the air, and the sounds of passing ships' horns cut through the late evening smog. It was unmistakable, and I knew exactly where I was. My old man, before he split, had taken me here once or twice to pay off some debts to the local union chief. It was a horrid place, and I had hoped never to come back here.

New York Harbor.

Vince eased to a stop near a pier on the far edge of the docks. Just behind some rusted old Maersk shipping containers, he cut off the engine and leaned back.

"Look." The single word was tense and to the point.

At first, I saw nothing, then slowly, a couple of men emerged from the darkness, each one carrying a wooden crate in his hands.

"Nicaraguans. Low-level scum that think they can move into our territory. We've been tracing their shipment of blow since it was loaded down south. These sons of bitches thought they could move product through our harbor without anyone noticing. Well, the boss wanted to send in a squad and turn them into cat kibble, but I managed to convince him to hold back." He flipped open a silver cigarette case, running the thin white shaft between his calloused fingers before expertly lighting it up.

"So? What has this got to do with me?" I asked suspiciously.

"You caused quite the stir with the killing of those Nomads a few weeks ago, and then the incident on Seventh? We knew instantly it was you. Word of your exploits has reached the council, and they are eager to see what you can really do, to make sure it wasn't some fluke and you didn't get lucky or something." A cold chill ran down my spine as Vince reached over and pulled out the pistol from the car's cubbyhole. Shards of yellow light ran down its matte-black finish.

"I want nothing to do with this. It was an accident, and I didn't mean to kill them. Just take me back to the Village and forget about me, please."

The Mafioso smirked to himself, tapping the cigarette's ashes on the steering wheel before speaking. "And then what? Work the rest of your life in the salon till you are old and grey? Maybe go back on the smack and be dead before you're twenty-five? Look at these thugs; at least with us, the trade is controlled, but with them, these animals have no qualms about selling to kids and those screwed up enough to snort their shit. You got a chance to change all that."

"And then what? Give the cops and Feds more rope to hang me with? That Agent Monroe already came sniffing around the salon, and he ain't stupid; even a blind man can see that."

For just a moment, a sign of recognition flashed across Vince's face before he composed himself again. "He's nobody, a pencil pusher barely out of Quantico. He's not somebody you should be worried about, and you will be well taken care of, providing you can pull off this job. So, what's it going to be, kid? Do you become just another dirty street greaser or do you take this once-in-a-million opportunity offered to you?" He held the pistol out tantalizingly in front of my eyes, tempting me to take it.

For a moment, I saw my old life again—the countless needles and strange places to crash. My drunken mother and scraping for an existence every goddamn day. Seeing those rich assholes in their fancy cars flying by, never looking back at the dirty urchin left behind between the trash cans of her life. Why should I not be happy for once? Why couldn't I get my own for once?

Don't do it, Charlie. Walk away; this is not your fight. Walk away. The voices in my head fell silent as my hand folded around the butt of the pistol. Vince nodded his approval and handed me a black balaclava mask.

"Get in quick and leave no survivors. Our boys in the local union will clean up the mess and take possession of the blow afterwards. And don't screw up, kid; both our asses are on the line here." Taking a deep tug of his nearly spent cigarette, he nodded for me to get going.

Slowly emerging from the car, I checked the magazine of the pistol and felt the cold night air on my skin.

Well, this was a stupid idea, I thought to myself, easing through the cavernous maze of shipping containers, sneaking closer to the men blissfully unaware of my presence. In my haste, I had forgotten to put on shoes, and my bare feet crunched Judas-like on the grey gravel under me. I didn't even have a clue how many men there were or what weapons they had.

One girl with a pistol versus a group of drug smugglers. Oh, nice one, Charlie. The tension grew by the second, the Latin voices mere meters away growing louder with each step I took. Easing around the corner of a sea-logged container, I saw the first guard standing with his back to me. Even from a distance, I could smell the product in his hair; it stank of oil and grease. Wraith-like, I crept through the shadows, appearing behind him. He barely had time to grunt as I clipped him behind the ear before dragging his limp body back into the darkness.

One down. Just keep going. I dashed across the courtyard,

running at full speed toward a nearby crane, making it without any of the other guards seeing me.

Need to have a better look, see how many I am facing. The dirty black-and-yellow crane creaked ominously as I climbed ever higher to the control room.

My luck finally ran out. A fat Nicaraguan emerged around the corner, sloppily munching a cheese sandwich.

"¡Alarma!¡Alarma!" he shouted, raising his submachine gun. Before he could react properly, I ran at him, hitting him squarely in the throat. In the instant before he fell, I grabbed his weapon. His panicked screams were coarse as he plunged downwards. The torch paper had been lit and guards came running at me from all angles. Gunfire raked the metalwork of the crane as I dived for cover. Leaning out, I returned fire with the submachine gun, shots connecting with flesh and sinew as my attackers rag-dolled gruesomely. It didn't deter them for long, and soon they forced me higher up the crane. Ducking and weaving between the metal railings as bullets came toward me, I nearly did not hear him creeping up behind me. It was an almost supernatural reaction that made me spin around, pistol appearing as if out of nothing in my hand, spitting fire and lead.

Double tap.

His skull exploded in a miasma of brains and gore as I looked down at my hands. They were as calm as death and perfectly still.

Don't let it take over. Keep it together, Charlie. A furious volley of gunfire forced me back to reality as I ran and dived for the control room. Barely making it as the glass window exploded around me, sending a shower of glass raining in all directions, I was trapped, and the ammunition from the submachine gun was running perilously low. Looking up at the crane and back at the controls, a gem of an idea formed in my head.

Oh, why not? A barrel of something was suspended on the edge of the crane's hook. It was the last roll of the dice as I madly started pushing buttons and pulling levers. The crane groaned and moaned at the strain of moving about.

"Come on, damn you!" I shouted, desperately fighting with the controls while the bullets ricocheted around me, forcing me downwards. Finally, I got it where I wanted it, slamming the release button with all my might. For one horrific second, nothing happened, then the drum fell to the ground as I watched in morbid fascination. A massive fireball erupted as the chemicals inside combusted, bathing the courtyard in a haze of blue fire. The guards thrashed around in a macabre dance as the flames scorched and burnt their bodies.

I silenced their choking screams, stepping out and taking aim with the pistol. Head shot after head shot rang out, each bullet finding its mark. Emptying the magazine, I watched as everything fell silent again, just the sounds of crackling fire remaining. Not a soul was left alive, the chemical fire burning away the last remnants of their existence.

Throwing the pistol away, I slowly climbed down the ladder and walked past the still smoldering fire. A container sitting by itself at the far end of the yard caught my attention as I walked over. Peering inside, I shook my head in amazement. It was packed full of bags of cocaine and more of the chemical drums, easily a small fortune in product alone.

Leave it, it belongs to the mob now, I thought to myself, smiling as I opened one of the drums before reaching for a nearby piece of rag, dipping it into the fire and throwing it into the container.

It exploded into a cacophony of fire and debris as I walked away, sending spirals of light into the New York sky. Vince was sitting quietly in the car, eyes wide with amazement as I climbed in.

"What did you do?" he asked, the cigarette temporarily suspended and forgotten on his lip.

"Being thorough," I replied casually, leaning my head back on the leather headrest and closing my eyes. Before Vince could say anything, we heard the approaching wail of police sirens and fire trucks. It was time to get out of there quickly as possible.

I don't know if he saw the slight smile on my face as we drove home, but I realized something, though I would never admit it to him. The dark side of me had taken over and I was savoring its power inside me.

I had enjoyed it.

The next morning, the courtyard at the docks was swarming with police from every precinct in the city. Even the hardened veterans had to admit they had never seen anything like it. At least twenty bodies burnt to a crisp and covered in a thin white blanket of pure cocaine, all with bullet shots through the head.

Through this chaos, Agent Monroe walked, taking in every detail and missing nothing. He stopped and bent down to pick up a discarded pistol. It had not been burnt by the flames, and he slowly sniffed it, turning the weapon around in his hands. The scent was faint but familiar, and it took him a second to recall where he had experienced it first. Smiling, he placed it in an evidence bag and walked back to his car. He had all the answers he needed.

The pistol smelt of lavender.

CHAPTER TEN

I wondered if was he was still angry at me for destroying the shipment of cocaine, but he simply sat in silence while we drove home, occasionally tapping his fingers on the faded leather steering wheel. Maybe he was thinking of how to explain several million dollars in blow floating on the East River to his bosses. It didn't matter to me anyway; I just wanted to get home and think about everything that took place. Time slipped past and the drive felt surreal, like a distant blur in my mind. I could see the men screaming as the chemical fire boiled the skin off their bodies, but I could not hear them. A morbid mimicry of death and pain played out in slow motion before my eyes. Maybe this other person, this other thing I carried inside me would not let me hear their panic cries. Was it a shield against the horrors it drove me to, or perhaps a bloody ice pick, hacking away at my last shreds of humanity? I had no idea.

Pushing the thoughts to the back of my mind, I eased up as we approached the salon again. A small light shone in the upstairs apartment as Vince nodded for me to get out. With a final shake of his head, he sped off into the night, leaving me alone on the quiet street again. I thought of heading inside, but there were things I needed to sort out with myself first. It felt like hours that I walked the streets, past shuttered-up shop fronts, some with forgotten and faded Easter decorations left in the windows, sitting with street musicians on the front steps of Capital Records, listening to their nightly incantations as they called up again to the gods above that had seemingly forgotten them all.

So I wandered through the razor blade night, finally settling down on the balcony of an empty high-rise building. With my eyes closed and my legs crossed on the brick precipice, I could listen to the city's voice again. New York lay before me, a firefly Rorschach of twisted light and grim night. Between the frenetic shouting of its victims and the gunfire of police pistols, she was silently weeping. Maybe this curse burning in my blood could be used for some greater good, or maybe just to bring order to the demons running wild below. There were no illusions; I knew the mob was pure evil, driven by dangerous and highly ambitious men. But they were the control, the constant factor against the animals pillaging the city for all she was worth. *God, do you hear yourself, Charlie? Do you realize what you are saying?* But I had no options left, and I doubted the mob would look kindly on me torching the Nicaraguan shipment. The best thing would be to throw my lot in with them and take it from there. I didn't like it, but it was my only chance at survival.

Slowly rising and staring into the neon-lit hell below me, I felt the soft May rain on my skin. It crept into every nook and cranny of my soul, washing the dirt and the last remaining shreds of doubt away. With arms spread open and eyes shut, I embraced it all, and then I knew this was the path I had to walk. My journey led through the worst scum New York City had to offer, there between the bloody razor blades and the monsters lurking in the shadows. There I would find and destroy them all. Maybe they heard my screams, felt it in their veins, a riot song of blood and steel, of death incoming. I screamed till the animals on the street stopped and looked up to the heavens, shivering as they pulled their jackets tightly over their shoulders.

A new demon, a huntress, walked the night and it scared the living piss out of them.

My walk home was slow and deliberate. For once I did not feel afraid, never having to check the shadows and alleyways. The rain kept sifting gently down, washing tattered copies of the *New York Times* and stained hot dog wrappers away. Electricity flowed through the veins of the city and it felt alive, like a heart brought back from the dead. I watched with detached fascination as the last of the night's dwellers ran for cover, leaving me and my impending thoughts of war with each other. Finally, I made it back the salon again and headed up the stairs. A small lamp had been left out for me as I reached for a towel, drying my hair off. Peter and Richard were fast asleep, hands reaching for each other across the two single beds. Kissing them both good night on their foreheads, I quietly walked back to my room and lay down on the bed. Sleep would often elude me on nights like this, as I replayed what took place earlier—every movement, every pull of the trigger revisited and analyzed over and over again. It all felt natural, like I had been doing it for years. An artist in blood and marrow, hands steady and unvarying as I painted the picture of elegant destruction, my canvas the blackened streets of the city.

It was difficult to focus on work in the next few days, and I would often make mistakes in the salon. But bless Peter and Richard, they never got angry at me, showing me over and over again how to set a perm or tie a ponytail. Maybe they realized I was working through things and needed all the love and support they could muster. We often laughed together, especially around the dinner table. Apart from his biscuits, Peter wasn't a bad cook, and he made the most marvelous red wine stews, often pulling out carefully hidden bottles of deep Merlot before Richard could find it.

And then, just as life settled down, he appeared again. We had just finished the evening meal when we heard the sound of a car's horn. Peering out of the second-story window, we spotted Vince sitting on the hood of his Lincoln, puffing away at a hand-rolled cigarette. Without speaking, I pushed my chair out and reached for my jacket. I didn't want to look back at the other two, too scared to see the judgment in their eyes. Having barely gone two steps to the door, I felt a weathered hand on my wrist.

"I'm sorry . . . I have to go." I turned around slowly and looked down, feeling ashamed. But they never judged me; they just standing there with calm smiles on their faces.

"Honey, you don't have to apologize; we know what you are doing," stated Richard matter-of-factly, raising a coffee mug to his lips.

"But how? I told nobody of my secret," I stammered, not believing my ears.

"Sweetie dahling, dearest Vince might be this big scary mafia guy, but he is also family, and you cannot keep things from Auntie Peter and Auntie Richard. When you started acting strangely and nearly left Missus Bedworth bald, well, we went over one evening to his place when you were out." Richard laughed giddily to himself as Peter went on. "You would not believe the unholy wrath two forty-something drag queens could bring down on the bitch."

"He sang like Maria Callas in two minutes flat," Richard chipped in.

"Exactly, and the dear boy told us everything about your nightly exploits."

"You're not angry?" I asked carefully, testing their reactions.

"Not at all, and we knew you'd tell us when you were ready. We're just going to make sure your white, fluffy little bunny tail doesn't get all dirty out there." The sparks of devious excitement danced in Peter's eyes as he leant back to Richard. "Be a dear and pass us the makeup box on the top shelf please."

With a quick flick of the wrist, Richard pulled out the stepladder from behind the door and scurried up the steps. Almost reverently, he took the makeup kit in two hands and placed it before Peter on the table. He nodded at me to open it as I eyed him suspiciously.

Carefully folding the plastic trays out, I pulled out a pistol from beneath. In shades of chrome and black steel, the long-barreled Beretta fit perfectly in my hand. It felt like a second skin as I marveled at its intricate craftsmanship.

"I don't understand." I looked up to my guardians with a mixture of wonder and confusion.

"We realized that we couldn't keep you from your nightly excursions, so we did the next best thing and secretly placed this order. It came just yesterday with a new shipment of rifles. You do what you have to, dear, but promise us you will come home safely when it's all over." Richard held my hand in his, eyes never wavering from mine.

I hugged them both tightly. "I promise. I love you guys." With a last nod at them, I placed the pistol in my belt and pulled my jacket over it. Vince was already waiting for me in the car. If he was impatient, he didn't show it and simply handed me a brown manila envelope as we set off.

"Your next target. Emile Lasalle. A low-level numbers runner from a rival organization that has been moving in on our turf. The boss wants you to deal with him but on the down low, so no fireworks this time, okay?" Vince stubbed out a spent cigarette and immediately reached for a new one.

"Why? Can't you lot take care of it?" I asked, paging through the black-and-white photos and essential information on the target.

"He's connected with a few local members of the NYPD, and it would bring unnecessary heat if our organization was found to be involved. But you, as a freelance contractor, will be free to operate unhindered and unconnected to us. A payment of two hundred dollars will be waiting for you at the completion of the contract."

"Seems simple enough," I mused, and closed the folder.

"It is. He has an office in a nearby factory, and my sources told me he is in today. Get in, clip the bastard, and get out quickly. I repeat, no setting anything on fire. *Tu capisci?*"

"I get it." The rest of the conversation was muted while I mentally prepared myself. We reached the factory barely half an hour later. It was a rundown sort of place, clearly long abandoned with a faded cat food sign hanging loosely above us. I thought it strange that the target would have an office here, but perhaps he valued privacy.

"I'll be back in twenty minutes. Make sure you are done." Vince eased the car away and quickly disappeared around the block.

Slipping the pistol from my belt, I pushed the rusty side door open and moved silently inside. The factory floor was cast in shadows, barely flickering light bulbs casting specters against old, corrugated walls. The only sign of life was the office light shining dimly up the stairs.

I should have been more careful. I should have taken my time. *Too fast, too fast.*

They came at me from nowhere, spine-chilling apparitions on me before I could breathe or draw the Beretta. I tried fighting them off, but it was all in vain. The ten men wrestled me to the ground, kicking and punching as I went down. A black bag over my head soon followed, and the world around me grew dark.

There was nothing but their sporadic voices and my heartbeat steady inside.

Calm, rhythmic, and in control.

In mere seconds, they had bundled me into a waiting van, the smell of burning rubber filling the air.

Keep it together, Charlie. Keep it together. I was going to need every ounce of my wits and spirits to overcome this.

I had walked straight into a carefully set trap, and whoever my captors were, they were going to make me pay for what I'd done.

That was for damn sure.

CHAPTER ELEVEN

The blood metallic on my lips, I felt the warm red liquid flowing down my bruised and battered face. Spitting a scarlet-tinted loogie on to the cold grey cement, I looked up through a rapidly closing eye as a fist exploded on my face, sending me reeling backwards. A set of hands roughly pulled the chair upright, forcing my head forwards again.

"I said, 'Who is your contact in New York City,' bitch?" My assailant had a thick dockyard scum accent, tainted with too many cheap cigarettes and shots of whiskey. His muscles strained under a much too tight white T-shirt as he leaned closer to hear my answer.

"Screw you," I mumbled incoherently, feeling the cold night air on my shivering skin. They took me to some factory God knows where, but I could hear the faint background noise of engines running. A cruel backhand ripped my head back, sending my eyes spinning backwards.

Keep it together, Charlie. Just keep it together.

"Your contact, you fucking bitch. I won't ask again!" he shouted angrily, drops of saliva landing on my cracked skin as he nodded to a second man standing to the side of me. His face hidden by a black mask, he immediately started hitting me. Brutal, bloody shots that would have knocked a normal man stone cold, but somehow I kept clawing onto consciousness, clinging on with everything I had in me.

"I'll tell you . . . I'll tell you," I said softly, strands of bloody spit hanging from my lips and chin. The man stopped and looked at me with glacier-cold eyes.

"Well? I'm waiting. Talk." The expectation raised the man's voice an octave, betraying his eagerness at finally getting the information out of me. They had been at it for hours, beating me senseless as a yellow moon shone dimly through the broken and cracked windows of the factory. The distant sounds of taxis and car horns seemed a million miles away, like I was on another planet. It was just me and these two bastards beating the shit out of me.

"It's . . . It's . . ."

"Yes?"

"The Easter Bunny. He loves it when you scratch his eggs. Go on, I'll wait for you." I didn't care that it was a mistake as he hit me over and over again, never stopping till my face was a study in blood. Panting heavily, the man stepped back, unsure of what to do. I smiled at him grimly, infuriating him even further.

Just as he was about to lay into me again, the one in the mask stopped him with a hand to the chest. "This is not working. She's not going to break so easily. Let's try something else." Deliberately taking his time, he slowly walked over to a nearby industrial wall socket and pulled it out. Orange sparks danced macabrely on the cement floor as he held the live power point inches away from my skin. I could hear it humming, buzzing with energy inside. He spoke softly, deadly and calm, picking his words with cold perfection.

"Who is your contact? You owe them no loyalty. Just give me a name and I'll make the pain stop."

"Go fuck yourself," I said, my words barely a whisper but laced in defiance as I looked him in the eyes.

Without remorse, he jammed the power point down on my sweat-laden skin. My screams would make a Valkyrie's blood turn to ice. Convulsing violently, I fought to free myself from the ropes binding me to the chair. Veins crackling under the strain of the pure electricity flowing through me, I felt the monster inside me come alive. The black poison ran riot inside me, screaming, wanting desperately to be set free. Teeth clenching, threatening to snap at any moment, I looked up at the masked man and saw with perverse pleasure the look of horror in his eyes that I had not yet succumbed. For a moment he hesitated, then nodded at the other man to turn up the voltage.

The pain was unimaginable, the energy unforgiving and cruel, burning my very soul from the inside. I felt death's shadow falling over me, urging me to cross over and give up. I was so close to the final release, so close I could almost touch it. But death would not claim me yet, skeletal jaws jabbering at my pathetic attempts as he stood watching passively.

And then it went quiet. The crackling of electricity fell silent and the room faded from view. No more pain, no more suffering. I was alone again in shades of pure white, walking through a busy laboratory, though no one took notice of me, like I was a ghost to them. Through the haze, I saw bodies strapped to gurneys, most of them children barely past the age of ten. Row upon row, with doctors checking their vital signs and monitoring their heart rates. A scene of pure horror as a boy spat bright red blood on his bedsheets, thrashing violently against the orderlies holding him down. Somehow, I knew he had little time left as he finally went limp, head lolling to the side, eyes shutting tightly. Without so much as a word spoken or a tear shed, they picked up his now-still corpse and carted him away. Body followed body in the same callous manner. Nameless, faceless souls never to be heard from again, it sent a shudder down my spine.

Hearing the soft moans of another child behind me, I turned and walked over to her. She could not have been more than a few months shy of her eighth birthday. Her long blonde hair draped in sweat as she shivered uncontrollably.

What do I know about children? I thought, placing my hand on her arm. "Take it easy, kid. Just take it easy." For just a moment she seemed to relax, her breathing evening out. Then suddenly, her eyes shot open and she broke free from the leather straps tying her down, placing a still-shaking palm on my forehead. The sheer force flung me backwards against the wall, and I saw something flash past my eyes. It was the symbol of the snake, coiled and ready to strike, venom dripping from razor-sharp fangs.

Then I started falling, falling deeper down an impossible chasm, the hospital room becoming a pinpoint of light in the far distance. In a snapshot of time, I had appeared in a richly adorned tent. A bearded man lay sleeping soundly, and I watched in distant horror as a woman sneaked in, a metal tent pole clutched firmly in her hand. She looked up at my ghostly visage, unflinching and unwavering in her determination.

With one precise and deadly cool move, she drove the tent spike through his temple, pinning him to the floor. Gracefully rising to her feet and wiping the blood from her hands, she tightened the silk scarf around her head and looked at me with ice-cold eyes.

"I am Jael of the Kenites. I greet you, sister." Before I could respond, the images faded away and I was falling again, the encounter so brief, so bloody that I barely had time to process it. Who was the woman in the silk scarf, and why did she murder that man? It did not make sense to me.

The next snapshot happened instantly. Standing on a cobblestone street, I spun around in amazement at the beautiful, whitewashed buildings around me. They looked old, very old. I could hear the thunderous roars of distant cannon fire and the ragged screams of a bloodthirsty mob. A man in a bloodstained white shirt carrying a red, white, and blue flag ran past me, shouting loudly in a language I did not understand. It was too late to stop him, and he disappeared around the corner.

What the hell is going on? My confusion was rising by the second. Why did the vision take me here? And where was here? I just wanted some damn answers.

And then I saw her.

She flitted across the rough cobblestones like a bird in flight, a red cloak trailing in her wake. In her late twenties, her features were elegant and classical as she hid her face under a cloak, rushing up the stairs of a nearby building. I don't know why, but something inside me told me to follow her. Cautiously, I moved through the large wooden doors and up the antique metal-railing stairs. A hushed silence fell on the apartment block, intermittently interrupted by the sounds of cannon and musket fire down the street.

Hearing a commotion inside, I eased the door open and saw the woman standing over a man in a copper bathtub. Pulling a dagger from her bodice, she sunk the blade deep into his chest, killing him instantly.

Straightening up, she pulled the cloak back and looked at me with deep hazel eyes. "My name is Charlotte Corday. I greet you, sister."

"Wait, please tell me what's going on! I don't understand." I ran toward her but it was too late. The vision had already started to fade away, pulling me back past the woman in the tent and the hospital. I could hear the children chanting as one while everything grew dark around me again.

"Follow the cobra's tail, follow the cobra's tail," they sang in unison till the sound of their voices died away.

And just like that, I was in the warehouse in New York City. The pain had returned to my body and the blood was flowing freely down my face. I knew there was a deeper story behind my abilities, and I was determined to get to the bottom of it. I could not help but smile madly, my purpose affirmed. These dipshits could do their worst, and it didn't matter one single little bit. The tears ran tracer-like down my bloodstained face as I laughed hysterically, rocking the chair back and forth. The masked man pulled back to hit me again, but a stern voice stopped him.

"That's enough. She's proven herself a tough and loyal soldier." A heavyset man with grey at his temples and wearing a black suit emerged from the shadows and walked over to me, handing his cane to a bodyguard. Running a finger down my cheek, he stopped for a moment and looked down at me.

His voice like a silk-covered dagger, he said, "So, this is the little hellion tearing up my city. When I heard you were the one responsible for destroying the shipment at the docks, I wanted to make an example of you. Luckily, he convinced me that you could be useful to our operation." He nodded at the masked man as Vince removed his mask but said nothing. I wanted to scratch his eyes out, but I didn't have any fight left in me. The Godfather carried on unabated, his face mere inches from mine now.

"It's simple. You will be my attack dog, and I will decide when to let you off your leash. You will come when I call or I'll put you down." He smiled for the first time, brilliant white teeth flashing in the yellow glow of the factory's lights as he stepped back. "Welcome to the Cosa Nostra."

The men seized me again and threw me back into the panel van. All I could remember were parts of the drive back and them throwing me out later onto the curb by the salon. I could still hear Richard's panicked screams as they came rushing out, cradling my limp and bloody body. I swore I saw a blond man in a trench coat standing on the corner smoking a cigarette, eyes fixed firmly on us as I finally gave in to the darkness and drifted off into unconsciousness.

They had opened Pandora 's Box and let the monster out.

God help them all.

CHAPTER TWELVE

It was the quiet moments that hurt the most, the times when I closed my eyes and relived the events at the factory and the vision over and over again. Bedridden for almost two weeks, being cloistered up in the second-floor apartment was slowly driving me insane. Peter and Richard had initially wanted to take me to the emergency room but soon realized that there would be too many questions asked about me. So they decided to nurse me back to health themselves, flitting in all day with bandages, water, and steaming-hot food. I had to actually chase them out when they got to be too much, but I adored them for their care and attention. God knows what would have happened to me if they hadn't found me on the pavement outside the salon. The trauma from the torture would most likely have killed me.

A wave of anger washed over me as I pulled the bandages tighter over my arms. Vincent and the goons who beat me up used me like a ragdoll on a string, taking me to hell and back just so they could be sure I would fit into their so-called organization. I wanted to make them pay, every damn one of them, including the man in the grey suit. He was the head of the snake and had to be left till last.

Easy now, you're inside their operation now; the time to strike will come, but on your terms, not theirs. The burn mark on my chest throbbed and I lay back in pain, staring at the white-painted ceiling. Soon, I would inject the poison and watch it eat them alive.

Richard interrupted my thoughts as he brought in some freshly baked bread, biscuits, and vegetable soup. Looking at me sadly but saying nothing, he turned and walked away. I reached out and held his hand tightly.

"Look . . . it's difficult to explain what happened." I hated keeping them in the dark, especially after they took such good care of me.

Richard sighed and sat down beside me, placing his hand on my bandaged leg. "We all have our demons to stare down; some more than others. All I ask is that you trust us; nothing more and nothing less."

"I just don't want you and Peter to get hurt."

"We old birds are a tough bunch. You try being gay in the marines in the sixties." He laughed softly to himself and then turned and looked at me. "Wherever you go and whatever you do, just promise me you will come home safely afterwards."

I nodded and looked at him intently. "Home . . ." Saying the word felt so damn good, but I was still unsure. "Is this really my home, the place where I belong?"

"Right here next to me and that sexy man downstairs destroying my kitchen as we speak." There was no doubt or hesitation in his voice, just a calm reassurance that healed my wounds much more than any bandage ever could. "Besides," he continued, "where else will you get the best biscuits this side of Brooklyn?"

Trying my best not to laugh too loudly, I reached out and opened the window above me. With a now-practiced motion, Richard sent the biscuit flying out onto the street. It thudded heavily on the pavement outside and rolled away.

"I pity the poor homeless person that finds that thing. Now get some rest, dear, and I'll come fetch the soup when you are done." With a calm smile, he got up and walked to the door.

"Do the names Jael and Charlotte Corday mean anything to you?" I played a hunch, hoping he would know.

"Hmm." He paused, deep in thought. "I think they were female figures from history, and both killers if I recall. Jael was from the Bible and murdered some king in his sleep, driving a spike through his skull. And Charlotte Corday stabbed Marat in the chest during the French Revolution. Peter simply loves those dreadful game shows on TV. But why do you ask?"

"It's nothing. Just heard their names somewhere before and I was curious." When he had left, I lay my head back on the pillow and closed my eyes, drowning out the city noises from my upstairs window.

Both female, both assassins. What did it all mean, and where did I fit into this puzzle? My head started hurting and I soon drifted off, the gentle afternoon sun lulling me to sleep. And yet still, I couldn't shake the images of the chanting children and the coiled snake from my mind.

Where would it lead me to, and why did I get the feeling that it was not the end of the visions? Not by a long shot.

My rehabilitation in the following weeks was slow and painful, but I gradually crawled out of bed and down the stairs. Every inch of my body hurt when I tried to move, and I often had to sit down to catch my breath. True to form, my godparents helped me as much as possible and changed the bandages every night. They even took me for slow walks around the block. Though still tense, the mood in the Village had slightly calmed down. The memories of the Seventh Avenue massacre had started to fade from the collective consciousness, and it was business as usual on the streets of the Big Apple. I spent the rest of my waking hours reading up on the two assassins and training in the downstairs basement of the salon.

Too slow; have to move faster, react quicker. Cannot afford to be caught off guard like that again; never make that mistake again. Pushing myself to the breaking point at training, often falling down in agony on the cold cement floor, I willed myself to get up again and again.

There will be no mercy, no second chances if you hesitate. The Beretta became one with my hand, a natural extension of destruction as the dismantling and rapid-fire shots became second nature. Inch by inch, the wild shots focused in till I hit the paper targets with frightening consistency, imagining that each one was one of those bastards that tortured me. I would never truly heal from my ordeal, and the scars on my body remained for the rest of my life. They served as a brutal reminder of what happens when you relax and drop your guard even for a second. My scar tissue armor would never be breached again.

And then, finally, the day came when I finished my

rehabilitation and was able to move properly without any more pain. I could feel the city calling me again, its pulse beating as one with mine. The fire burned deeply inside me, and nothing on earth could quench it.

The hunt began again.

Three days later, I struck. A group of the Dirty Ones, a local gang, had decided to set up shop in at the Shamrock Bar in Queens. It didn't take a rocket scientist to figure out they were running dope and hash from there, and it didn't matter to me that they were peddling the shit, but I needed some exercise and they would do nicely. The cops knew to steer clear of the place, so that took care of one obstacle. Just had to pick my time perfectly before I made my move. Casing the joint from a nearby office block rooftop, I saw the regular patrons had long since fled, leaving only the scum behind.

There would not be an innocent soul left inside.

Dressed in a long, black, leather trench cloak with black pants and a chain mail shirt, I checked the Beretta for the umpteenth time. There would be no room for failure tonight.

"Ahem." A voice made me spin around. Richard and Peter were standing by the door, arms linked. I started to make an excuse but stopped when I saw them smiling.

"Dinner at eight, young lady. We expect you back before then," Peter said matter-of-factly, nodding at Richard, who walked forward and placed something in my hand. "Something to keep you safe tonight. Do hurry back, dear." He kissed me protectively on the forehead and headed down to the kitchen.

Leaving the darkened salon, I caught the subway to Queens, mindful of the police standing around. But they took little notice of me; I was just another street urchin roaming the lonely streets of the big city. Just before seven, I reached the bar and looked around. It was one of those typically fake-looking Irish places that the tourists always flocked to. The block around the place was unusually quiet, like everyone knew to avoid it. A brute of a bouncer stood at the door, heavy gold chains hanging from his ox-like neck.

Calmly, I walked up to him and reached out like I wanted to slip him money. He only realized too late I had placed a grenade in his hands courtesy of Uncle Richard.

"Hold on to that for me, chief. I'll be right back," I said, smiling sweetly as he turned and ran down the street, still clutching the grenade. Taking a deep breath, I unclipped the Beretta and held the barrel against the side of my face, feeling the cold, comforting metal.

This was it.

Kicking down the door and rolling forward, I stopped in the middle of the bar, weapon aimed deadly true. About twenty Dirty Ones stood looking in awe, some with bottles suspended midair, others about to snort another line of coke. They all gaped speechlessly at the girl that had appeared as if out of nowhere in their midst.

Twenty broken and damaged souls.

Twenty souls I was personally going to escort to the gates of hell.

20:30 p.m., Shamrock Bar, Queens.

Captain Phillips, a twenty-year veteran in the NYPD, downed another handful of ulcer pills and looked despondently at the carnage around him. Blood spatter coated every wall of the bar, dripping down from plastic shamrocks and witty Irish signs. Men of all ages lay scattered gruesomely like a house of fallen cards on the floor, some staring lifelessly ahead, silent witnesses to the mayhem that took place less than an hour ago. The forensic crew had already started carrying some of the corpses outside to the waiting morgue vans. He was a pissed-off individual at the moment, being balls deep in the wife when he got the call from the station house that something had gone terribly wrong downtown. He angrily sidestepped a nearby uniform dusting for prints when he heard the remnants of the front door swing open. Special Agent Monroe ghosted past the collection of bloodstained bodies sprayed out like a modern piece of art across the floor, like he was picking daisies in the countryside.

"It's about damn time you got here. Look at this mess!" Captain Phillips remonstrated, waving his arms in frustration. "It's bad enough the animals are killing each other out on the streets, but this is a fucking slaughterhouse! Twenty dead bodies and one highly traumatized bouncer we found in the alley. It took the bomb squad half an hour to convince the poor bastard that it was a dummy grenade and that he could let go. You had better get me answers. I want to know which gang was responsible for this."

Monroe ignored the fat slob and calmly bent down and

picked up an empty round with a pen from his pocket. Smelling it and smiling enigmatically to himself, he got to his feet and straightened his cream-colored jacket collar.

"Not a gang hit, Captain. This was the work of one woman. The huntress is back, and she is looking for blood. Fetch me a drink from the bar and I'll tell you a story."

The story of the most dangerous individual in New York City.

CHAPTER THIRTEEN

Agent Monroe walked over to the bullet-ridden bar and selected a bottle of Louis XII cognac from the top shelf. It was one of the few bottles left intact, and he poured the amber liquid thoughtfully in a clear glass, always taking it neat with a drop of Sprite, damn the critics.

Henry's gym in the warehouse district, abandoned years ago. It was perfect—just me, a creaky boxing ring, and the resident rats in attendance. I felt the worn leather of the red Reyes punching bag under my fingers, the indentations where a thousand fists had struck over the years as I sat back and slowly taped up my fists.

"What the hell do you mean 'one woman'?" Captain Phillips looked around nervously, unsure if they were breaking police protocol or something. Wiping away the glass from the barstool and sagging down into the plush black leather, he fumbled for the cigarettes in his top pocket and reached for a nearby ashtray. The wife had tried to get him to quit, even getting him patches, not that the damn things seemed to work.

"You heard me, Captain. One female, barely in her twenties by my reckoning, was responsible for all this. It's not the first time the huntress has struck; oh, she has been a busy girl these last few weeks." Agent Monroe slowly let the expensive cognac run down his throat, savoring the almost metallic aftertaste of the Sprite as he watched the crime scene unit starting to finish up their work.

I hit the bag with rhythmic ferocity, hearing the creaking of the metal strut swinging on the roof. Every punch louder, drowning out the screams of the men I had slaughtered a few hours prior. I kept going till their voices faded away and they became silent ragdolls dancing a bloody pirouette as I cut their strings one by one.

"How the hell do you know that?" Captain Phillips angrily stubbed out another cigarette and ran his hand through his slightly greasy brown hair. He had seen a lot of screwed-up shit in his twenty years on the force, but nothing that could compare to the sheer bloody carnage he had witnessed lately.

"I saw the exact same MO at the docks a few weeks ago. You were aware of that right?" He didn't give the captain a chance to answer and carried on talking. "Same caliber cartridge, Beretta, but not standard issue, same target consistency. Over ninety percent head shots, but the aim was not true, the bullet trajectory often skewing to the side of the victim. And then there was this." He held up a spent cartridge and watched the copper glimmer in the dim glow of the bar's lights.

Too sloppy; you have to be more precise, more organized. I swayed in front of the bag, thundering a left-right combination into the sweat-stained canvas. They will catch up to you eventually if you are not more careful. The gangs can wait. Pick your targets systematically and take your time; your prey is going nowhere.

"Can you smell it, Captain? It's lavender, and I smelt the same faint aroma when that Nicaraguan crew got hit at the docks. Coincidence? Possible, but unlikely; the subtle nuances are too closely matched for it to be chance." Agent Monroe took slight pleasure, a perversion of sorts, at always being right, enjoying the look of incredulity on the police captain's face.

"Christ, what are we looking at here? Some sort of sicko serial killer? I'll have to check with organized crime, but I'm sure there is no known female associate in any of the gangland files."

"No, this was not a typical gang hit. Whoever she is, the huntress works alone, and there are no signs here or at the docks of any backup or assistance. All I know is someone must have done something horrific to set her off big-time."

My enemy was not the gangs of New York City or the scum that roamed the streets; no, it was the wealthy thugs sitting in their palatial mansions in Manhattan, thinking they could control me. My final goal was to set the mob and everything they cherished on fire and watch them burn before my eyes. I took out all my rage and frustration on the punching bag, my silhouette black against the yellow-tinted windows of the gym, hitting till the blood dripped from the white bandages on my hands.

"So what do we do now? I can put an APB out on this nutcase, but we haven't even got a description to go on. I mean, the bouncer outside hasn't stopped shaking and pissing himself since we got here, so he's no good." The frustration was mounting in Captain Phillips's voice as he impatiently drummed his fingers on the wooden top of the bar.

"Her methodology is scattered and random, like a frightened

animal that has been backed into the corner. There is also no pattern or reason to where or when she will strike, and like you said, she won't be in the system yet. You can double the patrols on the streets, but I doubt that will make a difference, you'll just have to wait." Agent Monroe ran his finger over the rim of the now-empty cognac glass, feeling the wetness of the remaining drops on his fingers.

"Wait for what?" Captain Phillips's patience with the agent had run out, and his voice betrayed him.

"For the next massacre. You got no choice but to sit back and wait for it to play out all over again."

I sat back on my haunches and watched the punching bag slowly move from side to side, sweat dripping down the bangs of my black hair to the cold cement floor below. Savoring the savage afterglow of the sacred silence in the gym, I found an inner stillness, a quiet sense of purpose again. There, between my heavy breathing and the scratching of the rats, I knew what I had to do. To play the puppet till it came time to turn on the master. Had to be ready when the time came; no second chances and no time for hesitation. I had to be ready.

"I'm not fucking waiting for this maniac to strike again!" Captain Phillips rose to his feet, slamming his fist on the countertop, rattling the remaining glasses.

"Listen carefully, Captain." Monroe's voice barely rose above its usual tone, but the acid was clear in his words. "This is not the usual drugged-up bimbo you drag to the station house on a Saturday evening. This woman is responsible for at least forty murders in the past three weeks. She is unstable, armed, and highly lethal." He got up and walked past the silently seething police captain, stopping to look over his shoulder. "Oh, and she's responsible for the Seventh Avenue massacre as well," he stated casually, raising his collar and heading for the door.

"Bullshit. How can you possibly know that?" exclaimed the stunned captain from the bar, not believing his ears.

"The bruising marks found on the bodies weren't male; they were female," he said softly, but it hit the captain like a hammerblow to the gut.

Unwrapping the material around my fists, I carefully ran my fingers over the bruised and bloody knuckles, taking pride in each scar, every subtle nuance of pain. Getting dressed and pulling on my jacket, I switched off the gym's lights and closed the door behind me. It was a long walk back to the salon, but I liked the cool air on my hot skin. When I finally made it back just before eleven that night, I was not surprised to find a manila folder pushed under the door. Instantly, I knew that the next hit was confirmed, and this time I would be ready for it.

The hunt was on.

Agent Monroe exited the bar and walked past the last remaining cops standing around, barely taking notice of them. He had more important things to do than worry about the competency of the NYPD, not that they would be much of a problem anyway. The poor bastards had no clue what they were really facing, and it was best to keep them in the dark. It did not concern them. He reached a phone box down the street and punched in a number from memory. It only rang once before being picked up. Nobody spoke on the other side of the line, the only sign of life a steady and controlled breathing.

"Venom One is in play. I found her; she's in New York City."

CHAPTER FOURTEEN

It was those moments, those precious hours before a hit took place where I could sit in quiet contemplation and rethink everything about to take place. The old me wanted to rush in and drop the target, get it over with, but there was an almost whispering voice constantly drifting through my mind.

Take your time. Slow down. Work clean. Where this voice of reason came from, I had no idea, but it kept making sense to me. There was no reason to piss off the local gangs and police force any more than was needed. There was enough heat going around without me pouring more oil on the flames. The slaughter at the Shamrock Bar was front page news in *The New York Times* for the whole week, with massive pictures of the crime scene splashed all over page one. Typical no response bullshit from the NYPD, I almost missed it as I closed the newspaper, sitting in a local coffee shop with a steaming cappuccino on the table in front of me—the tall agent with the square jaw and blonde hair, the one that came sniffing around the salon weeks ago.

There he was, just off-center in the main front-page picture.

What the hell are the Feds doing around a local crime scene? I thought, pushing the newspaper to the side and reaching for the manila folder next to me. It felt like I had read it over a million times, studying every detail, every subtle nuance of my target. There could be no slipups, no mistakes this time.

Work clean, hit first, and get out.

Peering out over my darkened sunglasses, I watched him exiting a Town Car across the street. He seemed jumpy, nervous as he headed inside a nearby office block. Never a good thing for a target to be paranoid; made them extra careful at the best of times. Two well-built bodyguards shadowed him, one by his side and one guarding the car. The bulges of hidden semiautomatics were clearly visible under their black suits.

This would pose a problem if they got in the way. I didn't want to kill innocents, choosing to spare them if I had a choice. Had to make sure it did not get messy later on. Flipping back to the dog-eared manila folder, I scanned the contents yet again.

Target: *Dr. Maxwell Schreiber. PhD in behavioral science and pharmacology at Johns Hopkins.*

Age: *37*

Height: *6'2"*

Weight: *Approx. 200 lbs.*

Marital status: *Never married*

Current occupation: *Police consultant*

Dr. Schreiber, after a meteoric rise through the medical fraternity in his early academic career, had taken up a post as a consultant to the NYPD upper brass, developing state of the art but highly controversial medicinal truth extraction techniques that had led to the direct incarceration of a number of mid-level mob enforcers and their direct superiors.

They were targeting low-level street scum, and it was already paying off dividends. There was talk of even more advanced serums in the pipeline, and it clearly had the Mafia council worried. The serum was wreaking havoc on the lower and mid-level operators, so the order came down for the good doctor's swift extermination. This is where I came into the picture. I had to dispose of him before he could hand over the new and improved samples to his NYPD contact. He must be close to the final product if the police brass had armed undercover cops shadowing him.

He was a creature of habit, religiously spending his time at the downtown laboratory he frequented, always ordering the same take-out meal every day without fail—Mr. Chow's stir-fried chili chicken with cashews and a medium coffee, two sugars, no milk.

Maybe the details were unneeded, but they kept me focused. It was the little things that would make my mission successful or not. I had to be sure of every variable, every possible element in the equation, leaving nothing to chance. It was not difficult to work out his schedule for the week; I snuck into his offices after-hours and accessed his diary. The same monotonous and soul-numbing routine day in and day out, all except for one specific day. On the last Thursday of this month, his secretary kept his schedule open from late afternoon throughout the night. He never took time off work early, so it stood out like a sore thumb.

New York Historical Society, May 20th. 19:00.

This had to be where he was going to hand over the new samples, a quiet and private spot away from prying eyes. It was the perfect place.

With the details of the drop-off confirmed, I kept the doctor under surveillance, never taking my eyes off him. Making sure he did not deviate from his schedule.

Exactly thirty minutes before seven on the evening of the 20th of May, I had taken up a carefully chosen position on the fire escape of a nearby building overlooking the Historical Society. All the pieces were in play; now I just had to wait patiently.

Is this the right thing to do? To execute an innocent man? I thought to myself. The gentle smoke from a Korean restaurant drifted upwards past the rust-covered fire escape as I gazed over the distant lights of the museum.

Block it out. Focus on what needs to be done. This felt wrong. All the other times I had killed, they were evil men, but this one was different. He had done nothing wrong, and I wondered if I was crossing a point of no return. Somewhere I could never come back from.

And then what, Charlie? Do you think the mob will leave you, your mother, Richard, and Peter alone if you chicken out? They would slaughter them before your eyes and leave you till last so you could watch. And besides, you made a promise to destroy the Mafia, and the only way is from the inside. Suck it up, princess. I hated when the voice in my head was right. A few eggs would have to be cracked for the greater good.

"Sorry, dude," I mumbled, checking the magazine on my

Beretta again. A few silver knives I had borrowed from Peter hung from my belt under my black trench coat. It was a weapons stash meant for a local mob boss. I had to promise to bring them back in one piece and clean of blood before taking possession of them.

The minutes ticked away agonizingly slowly as I replayed the museum schematics in my mind. I had to be sure of each step, each corridor, and each exit.

Leave nothing to chance.

Just as I started to worry that he wasn't going to show, at exactly seven o'clock, a black Lincoln Town Car pulled up to the museum. Dr. Schreiber was, as usual, never late, never early, arriving precisely on time. He was a thinnish, rapidly balding man with a pronounced limp in his left leg as he clutched the silver briefcase and hurried up the steps to the museum, followed closely by the two hulking undercover cops.

Take it slow; make sure. I ghosted over the street, Yellow taxis drifting past me as I approached the white-stoned building, briefly stopping at the parked Town Car. No tourists; my luck was in. I did not have to worry about civilian casualties. An elderly guard sat behind the front desk, watching a baseball game on a small black-and-white set. He never saw me appear from the shadows behind him. Gently, yet firmly, I took him around the throat, cutting off the jugular vein. "Easy now. I'm not going to hurt you," I whispered, feeling him struggle for a brief moment before falling limp in my hands. Carefully, and making sure he was still breathing, I placed him out of sight under the desk.

Next shift starts in twenty minutes. Got to move. The museum was eerily dark and deathly quiet as I moved wraithlike through the exhibitions, past intricate paintings and photographs of New York's early history, barely stopping past a marble statue of Lincoln in one of the halls. Were they judging me? Did they approve of the intruder in their midst? I could not help but feel that I truly did not belong here. But then I should have been used to it by now. Always the outcast.

Focus, Charlie. Keep it together, I admonished myself angrily, heading upstairs, nerves jangling at every creak of the old building.

Carefully prying open the ornate oak doors to the main hall, I saw Schreiber standing in the middle of the semilit room, silver briefcase held feverishly tight in his hands. One bodyguard stood by his side, the other taking position over to the far side of the gallery. Soft-stepping, I scythed through the shadows, moving from pillar to pillar, working my way closer to the target till I could almost hear their elevated breathing, feel the blood rushing through their veins.

First, the bodyguard.

A bald ogre of a man, at least twice my size at best, I knew brute force would not work with him. I struck from the shadows, hitting him with a perfectly placed nerve strike to the side of the neck. He never had time to scream or react, my fingers closing off his artery as I firmly placed my hand in front of his mouth and dragged him backwards into a dark corner of the hall.

It still eluded me how I knew to do this; it came like second nature to me now. Did it have something to do with the visions I saw earlier? Could these inborn instincts be directly linked to it? There was no time to ponder on these questions as another door creaked open on the far end of the gallery. A medium-built man with slicked-back black hair and glasses, dressed in an elegant dark suit, walked over to Schreiber and shook his hand. I did not know who he was, but something told me he was an important player in this twisted and strange game.

Show your face. Come on, fucker. Show me your face. I couldn't see properly from my position; I had to move. I had barely gone two steps when I felt a strong hand grip tightly around the ankle.

"Help!" shouted the bodyguard, his panicked voice ringing out through the gallery, shattering the sacred stillness before I could silence him with a kick to the head. Chunks of stone and marble pillar flew through the air as the second bodyguard opened fire, spraying the gallery with semiautomatic fire.

Dammit, should have checked that he was properly out. There was no time to think as I dived from pillar to pillar, bullets ripping the once beautiful paintings on the walls to papery shreds. In the confusion and chaos, the dark-haired man ran for the exit, never stopping to look back for even a second, like he had anticipated something going wrong. Like he had planned for it. Dr. Schreiber also didn't wait, clutching the briefcase and running madly down the hallways, sheer panic overcoming him in his desperate desire to escape. The second bodyguard fell as he tried to reload his semiautomatic, two pinpoint shots from my Beretta turning his shoulders into a bloody mess. He lay twitching in a pile of red scarlet on the white marble floors, but he would live; the man was only doing his job and did not deserve to die.

Now it was only the doctor left.

I could hear his terrified voice down the hallways, the anguish in his voice as he sought to escape his assassin. Through the dimly lit corridors I hunted him down, the predator stalking her prey, the adrenaline in my blood mixing and pushing me faster and harder along to make dead sure my target did not escape. Finally catching up to him by the main stairs, a silver knife flashed from my hand as he turned to beg for mercy, the weight perfect, the aim deadly true. It caught him in the upper left chest, the blade sinking deep in his flesh and sending him tumbling down the hardened stone steps. Reaching for another magazine for the Beretta and about to deliver the coup de grace, I heard the shouting of guards and the distant wailing of police sirens. They would be on me before I could reach the bottom of the steps. Watching the doctor scramble to his feet and rush for the exit door, I saw that he had dropped the silver case in his rush to escape.

Slowly picking the briefcase up and walking over to one of the windows overlooking the street outside, I saw the doctor running down the steps to the waiting Town Car outside, fumbling madly with the keys before jumping inside and starting the car. I knew he would soon be reaching for the flask of coffee under the footrest to calm his nerves. I coldly held up a small, sealed flask of Saxitoxin to the light, the clear liquid swirling in the moonlight. Paralysis would kick in within minutes, death shortly thereafter, either due to the poison or the car crash from him losing control of the vehicle. The doctor would not see the morning light again.

Target eliminated.

Escape would be easy; there were plenty of hiding places in the museum, and then it was simply an act of turning my clothes inside out and blending in with the morning cleaning crew. I would simply walk out and be gone before anyone even realized I was here.

Looking down at the case, curiosity got the better of me and I clicked open the yellow copper latches.

What the hell? It wasn't flasks of truth serum as outlined in the brief but a mask. Silver steel with two narrow eye slits, beautifully shaped and rounded to the contours of a human face, it was blank, with no discernible markings on the front. It was both elegant and frightening at the same time, its purpose to strike fear into the soul of whoever came before it. Slowly turning it over, my eyes narrowed and my heart started beating faster as I saw the symbol on the back.

The sign of Venom, the markings of the black viper. Same one I saw in my vision earlier. And now I had killed one of the men who could have given me answers to it.

Shit.

CHAPTER FIFTEEN

Days had passed since the incident at the museum as I sat on the ledge of the salon's roof, legs hanging over the edge and feeling the soft midmorning sun bake down on my shoulders. No matter how long I stared at the silver metal mask in my hands, the answers would not come to me. There were no visible markings, no signs of origin or even a date of manufacturing, just the still and ominous black spider insignia engraved on the back. Almost like it was taunting, mocking me from a distance, I thought of throwing it in the East River, anything to be done with it. But still I held on, knowing that it was the only link to my past, the only answer to who I truly was.

What the hell are you? I mused to myself, turning it over for what must have felt like the millionth time. The result was exactly the same; nothing had changed. Just the still, silvery gaze looking back at me, laughing silently at my desperation and anguish. Angrily, I threw it down next to me, hands running through my short black locks as I looked over the midmorning traffic in the Village, seeing the flotsam of people drifting aimlessly from building to building. A slight cough made me look around; Peter was standing behind me with two glasses of orange juice in his hands. Settling his thin, greyish form down next to me on the ledge, he handed me the glass and sighed deeply.

"I figured you would be up here; I just had to escape the house. Your Uncle Richard is busy doing his morning aerobics classes. I love the man to death, but nobody should see a combination of leg warmers and a leopard print leotard this early in the morning." He paused for a moment, tapping his fingers on the edge of the glass before speaking again. "What's up with you?"

I pursed my lips and showed him the mask, saying nothing, the glass of orange juice forgotten in my hand.

Maybe I expected him to be angry at me, berating me for the funk I had fallen into, but he didn't. Uncle Peter was his usual calm self, the center of my storm when everything went to shit again. When he spoke, there was no anger, no judgment or scorn in his voice, just a man that cared the world about me.

"What are you doing?" he asked, a thousand-mile stare in his crystal-clear blue eyes, seeing so much more than I could ever imagine.

"It . . . it just feels like that with every step I take, there are more questions than answers facing me. This damned mask is my only link to the past, the only part that shows I exist, and I don't know what I'm doing." Despondently, I kicked out at thin air, stopping when I felt Peter's bony hand on my shoulder.

"The only evidence you will ever need is beating strong inside of you." He pointed to my heart, smiling softly. "You just got to stop forcing things, my dear. It will come to you."

I wanted to be angry with him, but how could I be? With one carefully and beautifully chosen sentence, he had broken down my walls and shattered my defenses. I just shook my head and placed the glass down next to me. "But when? It feels like I have been searching my entire life without even knowing it. Just a few answers . . . That's not too much to ask, is it?"

"Of course not. We're all looking for answers in life, to who we really are. It took a family to reject me and years of abuse in the military to find my place as a gay man in this city. I'm fully convinced that if you give it time, you will find the road that leads to the place where you belong. You just got to have faith, sweetie."

"I just wish it wasn't so damned hard all the time," I said, smiling a bit for the first time.

"Nothing worth having in life is easy. It's a bit cheesy, but it makes sense, don't you think? Now come. Time to raise our collective roosters and head downstairs. I think Richard Simmons is just about mercifully finished with his routine. God help us all."

Feeling a bit better, I picked up the mask and followed Peter back down the fire steps of the salon. I needed that little pep talk; it did me the world of good. Now I needed to clear my head and put things into perspective again. When the sun finally set behind the towering city blocks that evening, I took to the streets again. Leaving the weapons behind, it was time to run free and feel the pulse of New York City beating in my veins again. Black cloak sweeping behind me, I raced up fire escapes, taking the steps three at a time.

Ducking and diving under ventilation pipes, vaulting over bird cages and sending sleeping pigeons scattering madly about, the wind was in my hair again. Sliding down a steel rail, I leapt over a building gap, landing gracefully on my feet and running farther on, the screams of the city becoming a faraway din of white static noise. It was just me and the focused mind inside, nothing else. I could forget all about my problems and worries for those precious few moments and push it to the back of my mind for a second. The junkies and whores out on the streets looked up and whispered to each other as they heard the rushing of wind above them. They knew the huntress was patrolling the city again.

I sat for a good hour at Gray's Papaya over a hot dog and drink, just taking in the people passing by. I could almost feel their dented but determined spirits, each one fighting their own private war. This was life in the big city; it carried on, regardless of people or events, like a surge of unstoppable energy. It was a weird thought to have so late at night but somehow felt appropriate in some way. Finishing off the dog, I decided to catch a cab back home. My mind was at ease and I felt calm again. It was amazing what a few words from Peter, a bit of exercise, and a hot dog could do to the spirits.

And then it all came tumbling down again.

I saw the flashing lights first, heard the terrible wailing of sirens around me, and then came the smoke, the terrible smoke. My legs felt like lead as I leapt from the cab, barely waiting for it to stop. And then I ran, faster than I ever had before, voices screaming in anguish in my head.

No . . . no, I kept thinking to myself as I furiously pushed through a crowd of gaping onlookers that had gathered.

How could I have been so careless? How could I have been so damned careless? The salon was a roaring mass of flames, yellow tongues licking from every window and thick, black smoke cascading into the night sky. The firefighters were fighting a brave yet futile battle to put out the flames, the heat driving them back time and again. I saw one of the EMTs attending to Richard by the side of the road, a blanket wrapped over his shoulders and an oxygen mask over his face. Rushing over, I saw the horror in his eyes, his face ashen with fear and despair.

"What happened? Talk to me!" I embraced the shaking man tightly, not wanting to let go again. He pushed me gently away and pointed at the roaring inferno behind me, still too overcome to speak. Then I realized what he meant. Peter was still inside the building. He hadn't come out.

He was trapped inside.

Without thinking, I turned and ran, straight into hell's waiting arms itself, hearing the shouting of the fire crew behind me as they tried to stop me.

"Wait! You cannot go in there!" I didn't care; I had to find Peter and get him out safely. The terrible heat was overpowering, the smog choking and vile.

Ripping a strip of clothing off my jacket and tying it around my mouth, I fought my way deeper into the rolling mass of smoke and fire.

Not here . . .Not here. Where are you? Peter wasn't on the main floor of the salon; he had to be upstairs. The terrible heat shattered a nearby glass blow dryer, sending razor-sharp fragments in all directions, cutting me deeply on the arms and legs.

Ignore it, Charlie. Just keep going. Dashing up the stairs, I knew the entire place was going to go up in flames in a matter of minutes. For some strange reason, I thought of the yellow curtains hanging in the kitchen, imagining the bright material turning slowly into ashes, the life fading from it with every second passing.

Then I saw him. Uncle Peter was laid out, sprawling, in the main hallway, face lying still on the smoldering carpet. Carefully lifting him up, I tapped his cheeks a few times, desperately looking for signs of life.

"Come on, come on. Wake up. Come on," I kept repeating over and over till mercifully he spluttered and coughed again. He was in a bad state but still breathing, and I knew I had to get him out of there with all haste.

"Hold on to my shoulder and don't you dare let go." Grabbing him tightly, we started walking out of the blazing building, step by step as the fire raged cruelly around us, the once pristine furniture glowing red with dancing embers. I could feel myself starting to weaken, the smoke threatening to overwhelm me at any second.

Keep going . . . Don't stop; keep going. Lungs burning, my world on fire, I dug deep and carried my stricken uncle through the scarlet miasma, finally reaching the door and fresh air, gulping in lungfuls of it. It felt like it played out in slow motion, seeing the EMTs and firefighters running over to us and dragging us away from the collapsing building. I heard the final, mournful groans of the salon as she took her last curtain call and crashed to the ground. The place I called home was gone for good, and nothing I could do would bring it back again. With tears streaming down my face, I saw them load Peter onto a waiting stretcher, taking him away to God knows where. With a shaky hand, he grasped mine, and I could feel he was weak, very weak.

"Take this," he whispered, and took something out of his tattered red jacket. I looked on, shaking my head in disbelief as they carted him off to the waiting ambulance. My world grew quiet as I looked down at the still-smoking mask in my hands. It was glowing red from the fire, the silver metal evaporating my tears as they rained down on it.

To my amazement, I saw something starting to change on the back of the mask. The heat had caused a hidden set of numbers to appear in the metal, hidden away from all eyes, just waiting for the right set of circumstances to appear.

What did it all mean? Did Uncle Peter figure it out? Was the mask the reason the salon got torched? So many questions swirled in my head as I watched the only family I ever really knew being taken away to a hospital emergency room, not even knowing what was going to happen to them.

An icy-cold feeling ran down my spine that I was responsible for all this, that it was all my fault. I should never have left them alone; I should have known there would be retribution for my actions at the museum, that the mysterious agency that was always shadowing my steps would never let me go.

They would drag me back in, over and again.

And they would never stop, not till I burnt their fucking world to the ground.

In the shadow of the burning salon, I made my vow of vengeance, running my fingers over the engraved numbers.

They were going to pay, every single damned one of them.

3 4 5 7 8 8 15 16 37

CHAPTER SIXTEEN

It was late afternoon in the pristine and sterile environment of the Manhattan hospital, just a few hours short of visiting hour. Not that it mattered to us; we never left Peter's side for even a moment. I've always hated hospitals for as long as I could remember. The incessant beeping of heart monitors, the smell of disinfectant everywhere, even the squeaking of pushcart wheels on the dull green floor irritated me. It was a place where hope went to die. No matter the sympathetic looks or encouraging words of the nurses, it always felt like Death itself was roaming the grey painted corridors, his fingers ever reaching out to touch another soul. Sitting, my hands in my hair, elbows resting on the crumpled white sheets of the hospital bed, I could not bear to look at Richard. It was all my fault. I brought this madness down on them, and they did not deserve any of the pain and misery inflicted on them.

You should have been there. Why did you leave them alone? You should have kept them safe, Charlie. It was too late for regret, but I wished with everything in my soul that it was me lying on the hospital bed instead of Uncle Peter. The doctors said that he had suffered second degree burns to the side of his body and was being treated for heavy smoke inhalation. He had been in for emergency surgery and was now resting peacefully, heavily sedated as I watched with a still sadness the drops dripping away in his IV tube. It was metronomic in its melancholy as a nearby patient wheezed and turned over in his bed. The worst was to not hear Richard sitting next to me. He had not said a word since the trip in the ambulance to the emergency room, not even when the surgeon came to explain the situation to him. He was a passive and pained figure as he sat, head bowed, holding on to the hand of his partner and lifelong friend. The silence was killing me, and I had to get away, even if it was only for a damned cup of coffee. As I got up, I felt a calm but steady hand on my wrist.

"Where are you going, Charlie?" Richard asked, his voice soft, the pain clear in every syllable he spoke.

"I need some fresh air." I replied, hearing one of the nurses coming in to check a patient's blood pressure.

"Stay." Richard looked up, and for the first time, I saw he had been crying. The tears ran streaks down his smoke-stained face. He had not even bothered to change since last night, pushing away any orderly or nurse that tried to take him away from Peter's bedside. His vigil was uninterrupted throughout the night and day

I sat for what felt like ages before speaking. "It's my fault." Biting my lip, I turned my head away, too ashamed to look him in the eyes. I waited for the bitter words to flow out of him, to hear the accusations and resentments that had been a staple of my life. But they never came. Richard squeezed my wrist a little bit harder and sighed deeply.

"It's not, honey. It's just not." He tried to smile, even though it was hard for him to.

"If it wasn't for me, if I wasn't there, then none of this would have happened to you." The tears were close now, my emotions running deep, and there was no hiding it anymore. Maybe I wanted him to hate me, to scream at me; anything would be better than the stillness between us. He just shook his head and looked me deep in the eyes.

"Peter and I, we could never have children. The state would never allow two gays to adopt a child. But then you came along, and you brought such life and energy into our lives, it felt like we were thirty again. So don't blame yourself. This was not your fault. Lay it all on those sons of bitches who did this, okay?"

"Okay." I nodded, trying to hide a tear from him.

"Good girl. And you know what Peter would have said to you right about now?"

"What?" I asked curiously.

"He would have told you to shut up and stop worrying. Now hug me, stupid." We embraced tightly, and this time the tears flowed openly. I did not care who saw or what they thought about us. I was safe with the only family I ever knew. When we had finished bawling our eyes out, I wiped away my tears and looked at him again.

"Okay, so now what? We cannot go back to the salon, and there is no way my junkie mother will take me back, that's for damn sure."

"If . . . sorry, when Peter gets better, we have some friends in the theatre business that will put us up for a while. They owe me a favor anyway. No, Charlie dahling, we are sorted on that front."

"Good to know," I replied, smacking my lips a bit before asking him a question. "And what about the, uh, storage supplies in the basement?"

Richard chuckled quietly more to himself than anything else. "Well, if the fire reached down there, half of the fucking Village would be having Mardi Gras down south by now. As long as nobody sticks his snout in there, we are sitting pretty."

"Good, good . . ." The sentence hung in midair as I sensed another presence in the doorway of the ward.

Vince and two burly men in black suits were standing stoically, watching us. Without thinking, I jumped to my feet and rushed straight at him, grabbing the big Italian by the collar and shoving him into a nearby supply closet. He waved off his goons as the lightning flashed in my eyes.

"What the fuck do you want?" I was beside myself with anger, the blood pumping in my rage-filled veins.

"Easy, *bambina*, easy now. The men out there are for your protection. Just to make sure there won't be another attack." He tried to push me off him, but I would not let go.

"Who did it? Answer me!" I did not care if I was causing a commotion in the usually serene confines of the hospital. I just did not care.

"It could be any of a hundred people you crossed. You have become very popular, young lady, and you haven't been exactly subtle, have you? We need to take all the precautions we can while I figure out who was behind the torching of the salon, *capisce?*"

"I did not ask for your damn help! I just want my Peter back, that's all. You had better find those who did it before I do, because I am going to bathe the streets in their blood. Do you get me?" I let Vince go and he stepped backwards, straightening his clothes.

"Just don't do anything stupid. Okay, *ragazza?* I'll tell the men to keep a respectful distance, but they will be near if you need them." He held up his hands and walked out of the storage room, stopping for a moment to look over his shoulder before speaking. "Those numbers on your hand, what do they mean?"

I had written down the numbers from the back of the mask on my hand before the metal cooled down and they faded away. "Just some betting numbers Richard wanted me to run before the incident," I lied. "Why does it matter to you?"

"It just struck me as a weird coincidence. They are all the numbers from retired famous Yankee players — Ruth, Gehrig, DiMaggio, Mantle, Berra, Dickey, Munson, Ford, and Stengel. I'm a bit of a baseball stats buff in my spare time." He shrugged his shoulders and walked out, leaving me openmouthed and stunned.

Could that be what the numbers meant? Was the next step to finding the persons behind the Venom symbol right here in New York City?

I sat down in amazement next to Richard, not saying anything as a million thoughts ran through my head. But inside, I knew what had to be done.

I was heading to Yankee Stadium, and I was going to find the answers to my questions.

Come what may.

CHAPTER SEVENTEEN

The cab ride to the Bronx was a strangely muted affair, my thoughts a million miles away from the midmorning traffic humming along the busy streets of New York, from the multitude of people drifting flotsam-like to their next destination. They didn't really matter to me, my only thought the strange sequence of numbers and their link to Yankee Stadium. Surely they would not have been so brazen as to leave such a monumental clue at such an iconic venue. Or maybe I was just not supposed to find the mask, and I had accidentally stumbled on their sordid operation. I just hoped that I would finally find some answers to my lingering questions there. *Get it together, Charlie*, I admonished myself and checked the Beretta tucked away in the inner folds of my overcoat for the umpteenth time. Luckily, Peter and Richard had a small backup storage unit for emergencies, and I could restock there without too much hassle. I kept thinking back to Peter still lying in a bed in New York Presbyterian Hospital. I didn't want to leave him and Richard behind, but something inside told me that I had to move on the information gained. There was no telling if there was even anything left of the organization, but I had to take the risk and go find out. I just had to.

The cab ride was agonizingly slow as I drummed my fingers on the faded brown seats. Maybe it was a blessing that traffic was heavy this morning; it gave me a chance to get my head on straight and think clearly about what I was going to do once I got to the stadium.

The Bronx. The goddamn Bronx. A fetid cesspool of vapid dreams and long-buried hopes. It was nothing short of a war zone as I glimpsed a gang of thugs stripping a car in an alley in broad daylight and a downtrodden man walking past the rubble-filled remains of a complex building. I was no stranger to the place and hung out often here, but it never truly felt like home, like a place where I belonged. Raggedy-looking women hung out the windows of apartment buildings, shouting profanities at passing blue police vehicles while the sounds of rap and hip-hop drifted down from a squalid and rubbish-lined street corner. No, it definitely was not a place for the faint of heart, and you had to be a special kind of crazy to live here. As we turned down 161st I saw the off-grey stadium looming in front of us. I was never really a big baseball fan, and I could not remember much of the place, to be honest. My father took me there one year when I was seven or eight years old, but it was something I chose to forget. He got wasted on cheap beer before the third inning, and the stadium security dragged his ass away when he got into a fight with another fan. I remember sitting in the police station, my father behind bars till my mother came to bail him out. I wanted to hate the son of a bitch, but he was never truly there, pissing off before my ninth birthday, leaving us behind to fend for ourselves. Good riddance, you piece of shit.

The stadium was eerily quiet, with only a few delivery trucks dropping off supplies for the weekend's games. Not many tourists had the guts to brave the Bronx, so I didn't have to worry about the crowds getting in my way. Security was also lax; I mean, who really cared about a teenage girl walking about?

Taking my time, I headed down the long and winding grey corridors, past the closed concession stands, and down to the lower bleachers. Putting my feet on the blue seats, I sat back and looked out over the pristine ballpark. It was a slightly overcast but still sunny New York day, and the field was looking green and excellent. I could not shake the feeling that I had been here before; not so much when my father brought me here, but something deeper, like there was an inexplicable attraction to the place. Like an unheard but still palpable voice calling me down into the bowels of the stadium. Taking my time, I looked for the exits, making sure of every corridor and escape route possible before slowly getting to my feet. A groundskeeper was steadily pushing a lawnmower down to third base, but he did not seem to notice me.

More by instinct than definite plan, I casually walked down to the elevators, listening for any suspicious sounds.

What the hell did you expect, some evil guys dressed in black coming at you in broad daylight? Don't be stupid, Charlie. Instantly feeling stupid, I shook my head and pushed the elevator button down to the lower levels of the stadium. The mask in my coat pocket started slowly vibrating as I took it out and looked at its cold metal visage. It seemed that the closer it got to home, the more agitated and excited it got, almost as if it were alive, sensing its origin was close.

What are you? The thought ran through my mind again, the answers so tantalizingly close, yet still so far. With a slight shudder, the elevator came to a stop, jerking me out of my thoughts. The foreboding tunnels lay before me, white-painted walls leading off into the unknown bowels of the stadium. Hearing a cough from down the hall, most likely an equipment manager or one of the players, I knew I had to move quickly now.

Not supposed to be down here. Just blind luck that security hasn't caught you yet. Holding out the mask, I let it guide me farther down the deep and immersive rabbit's warren. Past closed doors and half-flickering lights we went till silence wrapped itself around us.

The sounds of the stadium faded away as I reached a staircase, rarely used judging by the amount of dust settled on it. Feathering the Beretta, I inched my way down the steps, waiting in anticipation for a demon to jump at me from the shadows.

But all remained quiet. And then I found it. Past a pile of discarded advertising boards and broken seats, at the end of a dimly lit corridor I saw it. A keypad barely flickering red in the choking gloom. Running my fingers over the faded keypad, I knew I was at a crossroads in my life. The choice was simple: turn around and walk away, purge it from my mind, and hope to live a short but uneventful life till the corporation came for me. Or I could go through this door and finally find out who I really was—my purpose and my goal.

No, there is no more running away, Charlie. These bastards will never let you go. You have to do this. Hesitating for a moment, I wondered what the pass code was before looking down at the mask in my hand. It was humming, buzzing, and vibrating, its excitement palpable. Biting my lip, I entered the sequence of numbers on the back of it.

3 4 5 7 8 8 15 16 37

The thick metal door creaked and groaned, gears twisting and turning inside as it slowly swung open. Carefully putting the mask away and reaching for the Beretta, I felt the cool grip under my sweaty palm, the cold metal death trigger on my fingertips. Hearing the crackling of electricity and the starting of a far-off generator, I took a deep breath and entered the dark passageway before me.

Stepping out into a huge warehouse-like space, the bright spotlights temporally blinding me for a moment, I saw the symbol of the Venom Corporation painted in black on the far wall. Large and menacing, the coiled viper looked at me with bloodless eyes, taunting me to come closer. In a second, I felt his presence near me, like a wraith appearing from the shadows. Slowly, I raised my pistol up to the second-floor gantry and watched his calm and icy demeanor looking down at me.

The man in black from the museum. He was here. Waiting for me. "Hello, Charlotte. Welcome home."

CHAPTER EIGHTEEN

"Who are you?" I kept the Berretta steady on him, never wavering for so much as a split second as he sat crouched on the railing of the second-story pavilion. He could not have been much older than twenty-six, twenty-seven at best. Thin but not scrawny, his movements mimicking a coiled cobra, ready to strike at any moment. With nimble grace and a black trench coat flapping behind him, he leapt down from the railing, feet landing securely and softly. Oily black hair covered half his face as he turned away from me and looked intently at the symbol of the viper painted on the wall.

"A name? It sounds like a cliché, but we never had names. How many nights did I lie strapped to that goddamn bed wishing I had so much as that? It seems pathetic now, doesn't it?" he mused to himself and looked over his shoulder, a gunmetal blue eye piercing a hole through me. "You may call me Victor. It's a name I picked for myself — better than the string of numbers they printed on our files." His voice was bitter and sardonic as he sneered at me.

"What is this place?" My eyes narrowed in anger, finger

dancing on the pistol's trigger. Victor threw his head back and laughed suddenly, shattering the reticent silence of the empty bunker around us.

Finally, he turned around fully, and I saw for the first time the reason for his bitterness.

They took his eye.

"This was Genesis for you, me and all the others who they butchered in their experiments." There was no anger in his voice, just a chilling calmness that sent shivers down my spine.

"I don't understand." For the first time, I lowered the pistol slightly and started looking around me.

There was nothing left inside the bunker, just jagged scratch marks of hopeless and desperate hands on the once pristine white walls. With a cold and sudden realization, I knew there had been others like me. Lost, forgotten souls that spent their last days in this underground hell. For a moment I wondered what the last thing they saw was before death claimed them.

Why should it even have mattered to me? I never knew them; they were just empty faces to me. But somehow, in some weird and bizarre manner, it did matter to me.

"We were to be perfect in every way, shape, and form. The perfect killing machines, tools for our fucked-up governments to use whenever they needed someone disposed of. No links back to them, no deniability, no mess. If any one of us screwed up, then it was as simple as pulling a plug on us. Who really cared if they found another dead junkie in an alley in some godforsaken city somewhere? It was clean, it was sterile, and it was beautiful." The last word hung ironically in the air as Victor laughed softly to himself.

"Then what about us? How can we still be alive?" I asked, feeling my whole world collapsing in on me.

"I was the only one to escape the facility years ago, and as for you . . ." He paused, running his teeth over his lower lip. "You were the final evolution of the program, the pinnacle of their research. Oh, they had big plans for you, Charlotte; you were to be auctioned off to the highest bidder. They would have come from all over the world for the chance to own you—oil rich Arabs, The Russian *Bratva*, African dictators, Yakuza, Triads, you name it. They all wanted the perfect assassin for themselves. Well, that was the plan till something went wrong and they shuttered the program. I still don't understand why they chose to wipe your memory instead of just killing you, but it doesn't really matter to me." A disconcerting if slight smile had formed on his face, though he tried to hide it.

"It just doesn't make sense. I mean, how can this be?" I looked desperately at Victor for answers, but he never answered me, instead calmly reaching for a pistol in his inner jacket, pointing it squarely at me.

"In a second, you won't have to worry about it anymore. I want the mask, Charlotte. I know you have it." Victor's voice never wavered and never raised as much as an octave. He was clearly psychotic in his convictions and zeal.

"What's the mask got to do with anything?" I was stalling, trying to buy time, mentally planning my escape route. Pulling the silver mask from my jacket, I saw Victor lose his composure for just the briefest of moments, long fingers twitching in anticipation at the prize in my hand.

"It's so much more than a simple mask. It's the backup of their entire operation; all their genetic experiments, every piece of science and data is locked away in there. And it contains the Valkyrie sequence, the crown jewel of everything they worked for."

"What are you going to do with it?" I asked, inching my way around to the open door. Victor was no ally to me. No, it was clear he was in this for himself only.

"Leverage, simple as that. The Venom Corporation would not dare touch me knowing I have a backup record of their dirty little deeds stashed away somewhere." He looked at me intently, and I could see in his single eye he was just as lost as I was. "Come on, Charlotte, you didn't really think they would just cease to exist, right? True evil can never really die. They've always been out there, watching and waiting from the shadows. Who do you think torched the salon? They did, all to get their hands on the mask."

"You sons of bitches. I never wanted anything to do with you. I just wanted to be left in peace. Was that too much to ask?" I took a step forward, but the waving barrel of the pistol made me stop in my tracks.

"You became involved the moment they took you from the orphanage as a baby. You never had any choice or say in the matter, Charlotte, though I wish you'd kept your nose out of my affairs. I was this close to acquiring the mask off the good doctor at the museum when you intervened. In hindsight, I should have killed you that night, but I'll fix my mistake right now. Just imagine their reaction when I give them the mask *and* your corpse. It will be perfect."

"I'm sorry they hurt you, Victor. I wish I could take away your pain." My words suddenly seemed hollow as his once cool façade finally cracked and his anguish was laid bare before me.

"Pain? What the fuck do you know of pain?" he screamed at me, eyes wide, the torment palpable in his gunmetal blue eye. "They destroyed your memories, made you forget everything that happened here. They tortured me, day in and day out. Pumped me full of chemicals as they broke my body in training. I remembered everything! Even the night when I overdosed and took my own eye, gouged it out with a spoon stolen from the dining hall. I just wanted it to end, but you come in here and talk about pain? You haven't got a damn clue what pain is." A drop of blood ran down Victor's hollow eye and dripped to the floor as his hands shook uncontrollably.

I paused for a moment and looked at the tragic figure, actually feeling sorry for him. They used him, took everything he had before throwing him away like a piece of trash. I wanted to help him, but inside I already knew it was too late. Victor's mind was already gone.

"I'm sorry . . ." As his finger tightened around the trigger, I fell backwards, pistol spinning in my hand.

His left shoulder vaporized in a flash of gore and blood as the Beretta spit hot lead. Shots rang over my head, plaster and cement exploding around me. Why I ran, I'll never know. I should have stayed and finished him off, but something inside screamed at me that this was not the time to fight.

Run, don't look back, run.

As I ran from the bunker hidden deep under Yankee Stadium,

I could hear Victor's bloodcurdling screams of frustration and rage echoing around the narrow corridors behind me. Only my death would satisfy his lust for redemption and calm the demons chanting loudly inside him.

The hunter was coming for me.

CHAPTER NINETEEN

Don't stop . . . keep going . . . don't look back. Breath racing, I charged down the dimly lit hallways, hearing the whine of rifle bullets flashing tracer-like past me. A dirty Styrofoam advertising board exploded into a thousand pieces, raining white confetti down on me as my feet pounded the damp cement below me. Had to get clear, force Victor out in the open. There had to be stadium security around here somewhere, just to give me enough time to escape.

Why didn't you just kill him back there? I thought to myself in the run, turning and firing a shot into the dark. *Because like a dipshit, you forgot to take extra ammunition, you silly girl.* That and I just could not get it over my heart to kill Victor; he was just like me. Just another pawn in the Venom Corporation's twisted game. Had to get clear and get my head clean again. Just had to try to make sense of it all. A spray of cement sent me scrambling up the metal stairs as frightened voices sounded around me.

Get out of the way . . .get out of the way, I kept repeating to myself, praying that no innocent bystanders got caught in the crossfire. My worst fear came true seconds later as a stadium cop appeared before me. Spinning out of his grasp, I barely had time to look around as a bullet struck him in the back, sending a spray of bright red blood gushing out over the lower bleachers.

Shit, shit, shit! I dived down a flight of steps, landing hard on the cement. Back against a concrete wall, I peered cautiously around the corner, fingers gripping the handle of the Beretta tightly. Victor appeared a few rows above me, the sun reflecting brightly on the still-smoking barrel of his hunting rifle. His aim was still lethal with only one hand, as his left arm was now useless. I could hear the shouting of more stadium cops as they came running toward us, but Victor kept them at bay with a well-placed shot just above their heads. They were used to dealing with unruly fans and drunkards, but never anything like this. I could not blame them for cowering behind the distant advertising boards.

Shut up and move, Charlie. Find the exit. Crouching low behind a row of blue seats, I sprinted for cover again, a bullet ripping up the plastic seat centimeters behind me.

"Come on Charlotte," I heard Victor shout above me, "Just give me the mask and I'll end it quickly. I promise."

Checking my ammo magazine, I saw I only had five rounds left in the Beretta. I had to make each shot count. He was no fool and knew exactly what he was doing, cutting me off the whole time from the exits, keeping me moving till I had to make a dash for it out in the open.

"It doesn't have to be like this. We can fight them together." I leaned out again and fired a shot upwards, the bullet ricocheting off a metal gantry and into the distance. It wasn't a wasted shot;

I just wanted to draw him out, but he was very good, keeping discipline and staying out of sight.

Four rounds left.

Already, I could hear the distant wailing of police sirens as the NYPD closed in on the stadium. I had to be long gone by the time they got here; didn't want to be explaining to them what I was doing inside Yankee Stadium with a pistol in my hands.

"Don't make me hurt these people, Charlotte. Their blood is on your hands." Victor was somewhere above me, but I could not place the exact origin of his voice. I had to get closer. Taking a deep breath, I made a dash across the chairs. Plastic shards scattered in every direction as Victor opened fire on me, the rifle spiting lead slugs in my direction. A round grazed my arm, a dark red welt forming as I clutched the wound, scrambling for cover behind an advertising board.

He's out of the line of sight. He has to move. Taking advantage, I scrambled up to the next gantry, pulling myself up by the metal railings, my arm screaming in agony. *Just ignore it, forget the pain, Charlie. Focus on what has to be done.* I caught the briefest of glimpses as Victor ducked behind a concession stand, waiting for me to make my next move. There was no telling how much ammunition he had left, and I dared not get into a prolonged fire fight with him. Once my magazine ran out, he could pick me off at his leisure. There had to be another way of getting out of this mess.

"Can't you see they're just using you, Victor? Use your head!" I knew I wouldn't get through to him; it was just to distract him long enough. A plan was already forming in my head, but it was risky, and I knew I only had one shot at it.

"You can't fight the inevitable. Just give up." An NYPD officer came running into the stadium below, and I looked on in cold horror as Victor calmly leant over the barricade and took aim at him. "How many more people do you want to get hurt, Charlotte?"

"Damn you!" I shouted, but it was too late. The bullet streaked across the open expanse of the stadium, hitting the cop center of mass, killing him instantly.

Victor turned his attention back to me, and another round whistled high and to the left of my position. I realized that he had lost sight of me, trying to lure me out and reveal myself. Now was my chance. Sprinting down the aisle, I ducked into a nearby room, my luck holding out that it wasn't locked. It was an old storage room full of vendor equipment and advertising paraphernalia. A battered old baseball pitching machine stood in the corner next to a bucket of baseballs.

Perfect. I plugged in the machine and positioned it at the entrance of the door. Filling it to the brim, it started shooting out baseballs into the stands, the balls clanging off the blue plastic chairs. The distraction worked perfectly as Victor opened fire in their general direction, shot after shot ringing out in the stadium.

He's close. It was all I needed. Waiting for him to reload, running as fast as my legs could carry me, I ran and slid past the corridor of the concession stand, the Beretta cool and calm in my hand. For a split second I caught sight of the hunched-over figure of Victor, but it was enough, and I pumped the last four rounds into his chest. His shirt ran red as the blood bloomed out.

Gasping for air, he clutched his chest, scarlet running down his fingers.

"Well? What are you waiting for? Finish me off!" he rasped at me through gritted and bloody teeth. For a moment, I considered doing it. It would be so easy to kill him right now, take away all his pain and finally end his suffering.

But I couldn't.

Holstering the Beretta, I looked at him sympathetically and held out my hand. "Not like this. We can burn down their world, but I cannot do it alone. I need you with me, please."

Victor spat out a glob of blackened blood and wiped his mouth before looking at me. A pained grin formed on his face. "I thought you were stronger than us . . . Was . . . wrong. You cannot show . . . mercy. Venom will fucking . . . destroy you." He wheezed loudly again, telling me to stand back as I tried to get closer to him.

"Victor, please." It was no use. He spread his arms wide, the blood running freely now, and stared at me with his piercing steel-blue eye. It was the look of a man that had lost everything.

"I hope you are ready to face the darkness. Good luck and Godspeed." He smiled for the last time and fell backwards over the railing to the unforgiving concrete below. Turning my head in horror and closing my eyes, I could not bear to look. With the shock still ringing through my body, I slowly approached the railing and looked down, expecting to see a bloody red mass of a tangled and broken human body below.

But there was nothing.

Victor was gone and there was no sign of him anywhere.

How did he manage to survive the fall, and will you ever see him again? The questions bounded around in my head, but the answers to my questions would have to wait. Half of New York's finest was descending on Yankee Stadium, and I had to get out quick as possible. There was no way to explain the wound on my arm and the pistol in my possession. If I could reach a vendor van or mingle with the stadium staff, then it shouldn't be too difficult to make my escape. Pulling off my overcoat, I tore a strip of material off and bound it around my arm tightly to stop the bleeding. Wiping my fingerprints off the pistol, I wrapped the Beretta in the bundle of clothing and dropped it in a nearby trash can.

So far, so good, I thought to myself, walking around the corner, heading for the exit. I barely made it ten steps when I felt the cold barrel of a police issue pistol in the back of my neck.

"Freeze, turn around slowly, hands where I can see them." The police officer's voice was harsh and to the point, tolerating no resistance. Closing my eyes in frustration, I knew that my luck had finally run out. I was too lax, too careless, and now it had caught up with me.

As I slowly turned around and opened my eyes, I heard the soft drawl of a voice drifting over me. Looking up, I saw the man from the newspapers sitting on a railing nearby. Agent Monroe carefully rolled a toothpick around in his mouth while the officer handcuffed me.

"We have much to discuss, Charlotte, so very much," he drawled coolly as I was led away to the police van waiting outside.

Things had gone from bad to way worse in an instant.

And I was knee deep in it now.

CHAPTER TWENTY

There was an almost perverted silence as I sat in the humorless interrogation room of the police station, only hearing the muted sounds of ringing phones and idle chatter outside. I ran my fingers over the crude swear words carved in the cheap metal table. I was no stranger to the place; they had brought me in before for disorderly conduct and drug possession but usually let me go into the care of my mother, eventually. I hated this place, claustrophobic and soulless, another step toward the end of the road. There was plenty of time to think on the way to the precinct, the steel cuffs cold and uncomfortable on my wrists. I wondered what had happened to Victor and how he managed to escape the stadium with the police closing in. *Surely he couldn't be alive, not after taking four shots to the chest*, I thought to myself, but inside I knew that he somehow had survived and that he was out there somewhere. Flawed and damaged, he was my prototype, a perfect example of how those bastards at the Venom Corporation could take a person and twist him to their sick ideals. He was me, and we were just pawns in a game so much bigger than any of us could really understand, to be used as they saw fit. I would have to destroy him before I could get my hands on the puppet masters pulling the strings. I had no choice but to do it.

Then I thought of Uncle Peter still lying in New York Presbyterian. I didn't want to leave him unguarded for long, and my frustration grew with every passing minute. There was no telling when Venom would strike again and make an attempt on his life. I had to get out of here, and quickly.

Not bloody likely, I thought glumly. They had me at the scene of the crime, and it wouldn't be long before they linked me to the massacre at the Shamrock Bar and to the murder at the museum. I was completely and utterly fucked, and I knew it. My thoughts were interrupted as the interrogation door swung open and the blond man in the brown coat walked in. I never really had a chance to have a good look at him before they dragged me away from the stadium, but I took my time now, studying him carefully as he wordlessly shuffled a packet of papers, making sure each one was in perfect place. He wasn't what one would call classically handsome, but there was a rugged texture about him, like someone who spent most of his time out in the woods, not chained to an office desk all day long. He pushed a thin, if slightly oily, lock of hair behind his ears and expertly fished a hand-rolled cigarette from his top-left pocket.

Casual as I tried to appear, I could not help but stare at his hands: thin yet sinew-like, the scars and powder burns of a hard life lived evident on his rough skin, hands moving like an aged Las Vegas blackjack dealer. When he had finished and the cigarette was lit, he took a deep puff, savoring the smoke before looking intently at me.

"You're different from how they described you." He shook the red-hot ashes off and tapped his finger on the bridge of his nose.

"And who exactly are you?" I knew his face from the newspapers, but I wanted to hear him say his name. The agitation was barely hidden in my voice; I wasn't in the mood for games.

"Agent Monroe, the one who has been following your career with the keenest of interest," he drawled, the slightest hint of a Texas accent evident in his languid voice.

"And what career is that pray tell?" I asked sarcastically, but already feeling a cold chill travel down my spine.

"Oh, Charlotte, must we play games?" His playful blue eyes suddenly turned hard as steel while he rolled up the right sleeve of his coat. I suddenly thrashed violently against my restraints, the cuffs cutting deeply into my flesh as a tattoo of the Venom Corporation lay before me.

"You son of a bitch! What do you want from me?" I seethed, teeth grinding together in anger. The agent simply laughed softly and sat back in his seat, cigarette balanced precariously between his thin fingers.

"I must say, you have been most entertaining," he stated, pointedly ignoring my question before continuing. "The work you did at the Shamrock was crude but effective. Luckily for you, nobody high up on the force believes a woman could be capable of committing such an act, taking out an entire gang before they could get so much as a shot off. I managed to lead them off the trail and suppress any worthwhile evidence as to your involvement."

"I said, what do you want from me?" Fury turned to icy rage, my eyes narrowing, never leaving the agent sprawled on the metal chair opposite me as he calmly took the mask out of a nearby evidence bag, turning it over with great care.

"I instantly knew it was you at the museum; it couldn't be anyone else. You lost a lot of your skills since your training, but there was no hiding the work of a Venom assassin. It's something you cannot lose, no matter how hard you try or how far you run." He flashed a brilliant smile before blowing a smoke ring upwards. "The truth is, I am here to bring you back into the fold and get you working again."

"What?" I could not believe my ears, and it sickened me to my stomach.

"We've always been around, Charlotte, always working behind the scenes, shaping and forming the world in one way or another. The corporation had to go dark seeing as the last administration was less than welcoming of our activities, but now the time is ripe to emerge again. We are going to sink our teeth into the world's jugular again."

"And what about Victor?" There was no use hiding his existence; they must have known all about him.

"Victor La Salle was a science experiment gone wrong, an ill-conceived mistake in the early days of the corporation. He is a loose thread we intend to snip off very soon. He was never designed to live for long anyway before self-destruction, but you, Charlotte . . ."

"What about me?" I interrupted him.

"You were the zenith of our research, the missing piece to this puzzle that eluded us all. You carry the key inside you." The spark of deeply seated insanity danced in the agent's eyes.

"What the hell do you mean?"

"Your genetics. We tried experimenting on others, but the process always failed consistently. It simply would not take with male genes, and it rejected most female genes as well—that is, till we found you. There is something truly remarkable and unique in your DNA, the catalyst that makes everything possible. For the first time, we could create the perfect assassin, flawless in every way."

"Then why did you let me go?" I was stalling for time, trying to escape the cuffs, but it was of no use; they held firm against my struggles.

"Political pressure. As I said, the risk was simply too high to keep the operation running. But we placed you in foster care as a child for safekeeping here in New York City. I'll admit that we lost track of you for a while, fluctuations of a big city and all that, but when dead bodies started popping up all over the city, it didn't take us long to figure out it was you." Agent Monroe had a self-satisfied smile on his face as he ran his finger over the metal edge of the table.

"So now what? You cannot touch me; I'm in police custody in case you haven't noticed," I replied.

"A mere formality, Charlotte. I will arrange for your transfer to an FBI holding facility at Quantico, but you will never reach it. You and the mask will be transported to a Venom facility upstate that has just been brought back online and you will be safe with us again."

"Safe." The word was bitter and acid-like in my mouth as I repeated it slowly to the agent.

"It will be like nothing has changed. We will wipe your memory again and then extract that oh-so-precious genetic code from your body. You are not expected to survive, but it doesn't matter in the end.

"Once we have your DNA, we can create hundreds, thousands of soldiers and assassins like you. Just imagine what governments all over the world would pay for access to that kind of power—and the leverage we would have over them would be immense."

"That's sick." I spat the words at him. "You cannot control the world like this."

Agent Monroe laughed softly, stubbing out the last of his cigarette. "We're not going to control it; you are, Charlotte. Every time blood is spilled or a political figure is gunned down it will be your genetic legacy that caused it. You are genesis to a new age of Venom, one where we become sentient to every political thought and action for the next hundred years. You should feel honored."

"Stick it up your ass. I never wanted this." My words cut deep, but if it affected Monroe, he did well to hide it, pushing his chair away and heading for the door. He paused and looked over his shoulder at me.

"You never had a choice, and you won't remember any of this when we are done with you. We are on the verge of an impossibly bright future. Welcome home, Charlotte." He smiled for the last time, placed a toothpick in his mouth, and quietly exited the room. My fingernails dug deep into the palms of my hands till a thin stream of blood ran red over the steel cuffs. I had finally run out of luck and options.

Nowhere to run and nowhere to hide anymore.

I looked on with resignation as two police officers walked in and unlocked my handcuffs and shackled my wrists and ankles before slowly marching me in my orange jumpsuit through the police precinct. I kept my head up, defiant, looking every cop, every criminal, and every civilian in the station straight in the eyes. Everyone became quiet as they witnessed the strange sight of two burly cops escorting a young girl chained in irons from the station. A black, unmarked van was waiting for us, and they bundled me in, locking my chains to the floor.

When the metal door slammed shut and the inky black void enveloped me, I finally let go and cried my heart out. Cried till I had nothing left inside and the tears ran down on my cheeks.

In the darkness, I had become truly alone.

CHAPTER TWENTY-ONE

What was I supposed to do? Scream, rant, and rave? Bang my fists on the metal walls till the blood ran over my fists?

Not much good it would do anyway. I tugged gently at the metal chains bound to my wrists, shook my head in disbelief, then sat back and closed my eyes.

There was no escape, no more running for me—just the end of a long and dammed road. What was waiting for me when the road finally ran out? Did I even have to ask? A mind wiped clean, a new life, or just another science experiment locked away by the Venom Corporation to unleash when they saw fit?

Not much of a life. In the darkness of the van, I thought of Peter and Richard and how I would never see them again. It was very unlike me to be this sentimental, but I missed them, no use in denying that. In a short space of time, they had become the only family I had ever truly known.

Dammit, I hope they are okay. I hated leaving them behind so suddenly, but I had no choice. There was no telling how long the trail of the mask would last before going cold. Fat lot of good it did me in the end. Like a dipshit, I had to reason with Victor instead of escaping. And now I was sitting here, awaiting my fate at the hands of these fuckers.

Well done, Charlie; oh, very well done. And then for some reason, sitting in the humid atmosphere of the van, hearing the diesel engine rumbling along and the grating of the tires on asphalt, I thought of my mother.

I wondered if the bitch actually realized I was gone by now. Most likely she was still stoned out of her mind, lying drooling on some stranger's floor. I couldn't help but suppress an ironic smile. I hated her for never being there for me; never being a mother; hell, for lying about me being her child. She wasn't even my own flesh and blood. *Screw her, she's nothing to you.* Just another ghost passing by.

How long had we been driving? There was no telling time in the claustrophobic darkness of the panel van—no day, no night, just the quiet rattle of rubber on the tar. A few minutes later, the van came to a standstill with a jolt, throwing me hard against the metal wall.

Holding my aching head, I heard the van door creak open, the sunlight suddenly harsh on my eyes.

"Sit dead still, not a movement," a voice behind a shotgun barked as another agent or whatever the hell they were climbed inside the van and unlocked my leg chains before shoving me outside to the ground. As I looked up from the dust, the other agent lifted my bloodied chin with his shotgun and looked me straight in the eyes.

"Bathroom break. We don't want you pissing all over the floor." He snorted behind his black balaclava as I dusted myself off best as I could.

"I know your stench, fucker; pray I don't get loose here." I smiled through bloody teeth, paying dearly for my stubborn resistance as a shotgun butt exploded in my back, driving the air from my lungs. As I stumbled toward the abandoned petrol station, kicking up dirt; the agent shoved me through the whitewashed door and into the restroom. The place was a filth-ridden mess, rolls of wet toilet paper laying in pools of water and broken mirrors all around. The stall itself looked like it came straight out of a Hollywood horror movie, but I had no choice in the matter. I looked at the once semi-proud remains of the toilet and then back to the agent, smiling as sweetly as I could at him, holding out the chains on my wrists.

"Only on the second date, sweetie." The agent rolled his eyes under his balaclava but unlocked my shackles and pointed to the stall.

"You have three minutes before I drag you out of there, finished or not," he hissed and stepped back, shotgun draped across his arms. Pulling the stall door closed as best I could, I quickly took in my surroundings, trying to find an escape route.

The bars on the window . . . rusted . . . maybe you can pull them down. The bars were nothing more than decorations at this moment in life, rotted away from years of damp and rust. Carefully, I laid them down on the broken toilet seat one by one before easing my head and shoulders through the gap.

I did not get far, my luck running out almost immediately. A rifle was pointed squarely at my head, another agent calmly waiting for me at the back of the building. I smiled sarcastically and threw him a middle finger before inching my way back into the stall. Sitting for a moment, hearing the metronomic dripping of water in the nearby sink, I knew there was no chance at escape. They had anticipated my every move and every thought. It wasn't long before I was shackled again and bundled back into the waiting van. The red afternoon light faded away as the doors slammed shut behind me again.

My last chance had gone.

Sitting in the dark, I could feel the mask near me.

It was vibrating and pulsating with energy, locked away in the passenger side glove box. Calling to me, its unholy yearning was palpable, beating as one with my pulse as I placed a hand on the metal dividing wall. It wanted me to know its answers, its deepest secrets hidden away. With grim realization, the thought occurred to me that I would never be reunited with the strange mask again, that everything it knew would stay fingertips away from me.

What are you doing? It's just going to drag you deeper into this mess you're in. I knew it was wrong, but I could not silence the voice in my head. The voice that screamed at me to follow the rabbit hole as far as it dared take me, to figure out who I truly was. It was the only way.

And if you find out who you really are? Could you live with yourself? I could honestly not answer that question, and it scared me. It scared the life out of me.

The hours ticked slowly by, and I had long ago stopped trying to figure out where we were. All I knew was that it was somewhere quiet and off the beaten path. I hadn't heard any cars for the past half hour, and I felt the van shake like it was on a dirt road. Where the hell were they taking me?

Twenty-odd minutes later, by my reckoning, the van lurched to a stop again and I sat deathly still inside waiting for something to happen.

Come on, come on. The van doors swung open and a spotlight shone inside, temporally blinding me. Holding my hand up to my eyes, I felt a couple of hands unlock my chains and drag me outside. The night wind was cool on my skin, my feet crunching on rough tarmac. When my eyes adjusted to the light, I looked around in amazement, scarcely believing what I was seeing. We had arrived at an abandoned airstrip, miles from any sort of civilization, and a C-27J Spartan military cargo plane was already waiting for us. I had underestimated Venom's capabilities; they must have a lot of clout to be able to swing this. There was no telling what reach they had.

"Move!" the first agent commanded, pushing me roughly in the back toward another group of ten masked agents waiting by the plane, its propellers beating rapidly in the glow of the spotlights on it. I knew the moment I stepped on that plane that I was dead; there was no doubt about it. But I had no choice; the men with rifles trained on me tolerated no resistance, and I wouldn't last two seconds if I tried to fight back. With a heavy heart, I stumbled up the plane ramp, the ominous and cavern-like space folding itself around me as I sat down.

"Buckle up. You'll be out of our hair in a couple of hours. Then you will be someone else's problem," the agent shouted over the din of the engines. I stared blankly at him as they strapped me in tightly. The hydraulic ramp slowly pulled up and I could feel the plane accelerating down the runway. The men around me were tense, not relaxing for even a moment. I wanted to see their faces, to know the cowards behind the masks. What did it even matter? Yet, somehow, it did to me.

"We got a problem." The pilot eased the throttle back and looked back at the cargo hold as the other agents readied their weapons. A group of black cars had appeared out of the night, blocking the plane from taking off. With a screech of rubber on tarmac, the plane shuddered to a halt, the pilot fighting to regain control of the large cargo carrier. More black cars came racing from the shadows, surrounding us.

"Move! Move!" The agents ran down the ramp as the night lit up with the sound of gunfire, the world exploding around me in a miasma of steel, blood, and gore. Black-masked agents fell at my feet, bullets ricocheting, slamming into the metal behind me.

It was an ambush.

The agents never had a chance, cut down one by one like cornstalks in a field of wheat. Some fought their way to the nearby vans, running and shooting through the chaos. A man in a black mask came running at me up the ramp, bolt cutters in hand.

"Sit still. I'm not here to hurt you. Are you injured?" he shouted as I shook my head before he cut my chains free and dragged me out of the plane. "Keep your head down!" He let fly with a burst of automatic gunfire as we ran for the safety of a waiting car. We had barely made it there when I grabbed his arm suddenly, hesitating.

"I forgot something. Just give me a moment!" I shouted and ran to the van where I was locked up mere moments ago.

"Dammit, Charlie, we haven't got time for this!" the man in black screamed, turning and emptying another magazine at the cowering agents. In the confusion, it didn't register with me how the man knew my name and how he even came to be here.

It doesn't matter, just get the mask. Can't leave without it. I reached the van in record time, yanking open the passenger side door and opening the glove box. Mercifully, the mask was still there, and I grabbed it and held it tightly to my chest. As I was about to leave, I heard a pitiful moan from the other side of the van.

The first agent, the one that had hit and abused me, was lying in a pool of blood on the tarmac. It was him, his stench unmistakable. I smiled to myself, reaching down and patting him on the cheek.

"Told you I would get loose, sweetie." Before he could react, I drop-kicked him as hard I could in the balls, taking perverse pleasure in his immense pain while I ran back to the car. The man in black pulled me into the back seat and the car roared off into the night, the cargo plane exploding in a fiery orange ball of flame behind us. When we were well clear of the airport, I sat up and caught my breath again, turning toward the man.

"Who are you?" I asked, eyes wide with shock.

"*Familia,* Charlie. We take care of our own."

Vince pulled off his mask as I shook my head in wonder.

"I don't believe it. I just don't believe it," I whispered, more to myself than anyone else.

"You best believe it, *bambina*. Now, keep your head down. Once we're clear, you and I need to have a serious talk. You've started a shitstorm of epic fucking proportions, and I got to know exactly what we're facing and when it's about to hit."

A storm that was going to turn New York City into a bloodbath.

God help us all.

CHAPTER TWENTY-TWO

"Vince . . . I . . ." There were so many jumbled thoughts racing through my head that I didn't know where they started and where it stopped. The adrenaline was still pumping in my veins, the glow of the burning cargo plane still an orange haze on the horizon as the Lincoln Town Car tore down the empty highway. I still couldn't believe the big Italian had actually managed to find and rescue me. The old stubborn streak was still inside me though, that thought I didn't need anyone to rescue me.

But I'm damn glad you did, I thought to myself, not sharing the sentiment with Vince as he looked over his shoulder for what seemed like the millionth time.

"Not here, *bambina*. We will talk soon." He eyed the young driver up front suspiciously, settling back in the plush seats of the Lincoln and exhaling deeply. I could see that the events at the airport had him spooked, as he was constantly checking the rearview mirror for any signs of pursuers. The night remained empty and treacherously quiet, the silence balanced on a knifepoint. The only witnesses were the ghosts of willowy grey trees flashing sporadically past us. Vince said nothing further, but it seemed like he knew where he was going.

About roughly an hour and a half later, he tapped the driver on the shoulder and motioned to him to turn down a hidden dirt road. The two cars behind us in the convoy turned with us, dimming their lights. A short drive later, an imposing farmhouse appeared across the ridge, porch lights lit and shining dimly in the cool breeze of the late night. Four armed guards, each one with an AK47 in hand, waved us through.

Parking in a straight line in front of the main building, Vince quickly got out, his instructions precise and clear.

"I want everyone on their toes. Patrols every ten minutes around the property and stay in contact with the guards at the gate. Are we clear?" The group of men nodded and left to take up their positions. "Come, Charlie, it's safe inside." Looking around one last time, I followed Vince inside. The farmhouse was elegant if slightly rustic, a typical hideaway for someone getting away from the city life. I settled into a faded brown recliner as he took off his coat and headed to the kitchen. It wasn't long before he returned with two steaming cups of coffee in hand. Gratefully, I accepted, the steaming-hot liquid instantly calming me down again. Draining the cup, not caring if it burnt me or not, I finished and finally looked up at Vince as he studied me intently.

"Care to explain?" I asked, trying very hard to hide the suspicion in my voice.

The big Italian paused for a moment, picking his words carefully, leaning forward to me. "When we heard through the police scanner of the shootout at Yankee Stadium, we instantly knew it was you, Charlie. Nobody else can cause that much chaos in such a short time. But I thought I told you to lay low, didn't I?"

"I had no choice; someone was already waiting for me there," I replied, hesitant to share the whole story with him.

"However it may be, there wasn't enough time to intercept and free you from police custody. We thought we had lost you when the FBI got involved. But something just didn't seem right to me."

"What?"

"Our contact inside the NYPD said you were being interrogated by an Agent Monroe. But there is no record of such an agent ever existing . . . What? You didn't think we would have connections inside the bureau?" he scoffed incredulously at me.

"Guess not."

"All it took was one phone call to confirm my suspicions, and then came the final nail in the coffin. They were supposed to take you south to Virginia, but they were heading completely in the wrong direction. That is when I rounded up the boys to make the save. Lucky we arrived when we did; once you were airborne, you would have been out of our reach."

"But how did you know about the airstrip, and why me? What makes me so special to make all this effort and risk so many lives?" I asked.

"One of my men grew up in the countryside and he pinpointed the location for us. It was the only possible way of getting you quickly and quietly out of state, so we took a chance and got lucky. As for why, the boss seems to think you are important or something, so who am I to argue?" He stopped for a moment, gently biting his lower lip, trying to read my body language. "Tell me, *bambina*, what do you know of an organization called 'Venom'?"

I nearly dropped the porcelain cup, fighting to keep the bile down in my throat. How could he have possibly known about the corporation? It was just not possible. "What . . . what do you mean?" I knew it was a stupid bluff, one that Vince saw through before I even had a chance to finish the sentence.

"Come on, don't play games with me, child. I saw the snake tattoo on the forearm of one of the agents back at the airstrip. For decades, Venom was a myth; a ghost story the old Mafioso told the young ones. It was scarcely believable, a shadow organization that operated in New York City right under the nose of the Cosa Nostra. I always dismissed the idea as the paranoid ramblings of men that had lived the life for too long, but I kept hearing mentions of them in the underground. The markings on the agent's arm were the final confirmation that the impossible had become real. I just can't figure out where you come into the picture." He sat back in the white rocking chair, shaking his head in disbelief.

The time had come to come clean; there was no use in hiding anything anymore. Taking a deep breath, the words flowed from my mouth. "They seem to think I am carrying some sort of genetic code in me, a blueprint for the perfect assassin. It's fucking nuts! I'm just a normal girl from Brooklyn, for God's sake."

"A girl that took out an entire gang in a heartbeat, one that is proficient in all types of weapons, tactics, and unarmed combat?

Doesn't seem very normal to me," Vince replied dryly.

"I don't care; I just want these assholes off my ass and to leave me alone!" I threw the cup with all my might and it hurtled through the air, smashing it into a thousand pieces on the far wall. Vince was unperturbed, taking a thin unfiltered cigarette from his top pocket and casually lighting it.

"You got no choice in the matter, Charlie. Like it or not, you are in it for the long haul." His calmness was maddening as I got up from the chair, pacing up and down the polished wooden floor.

"So now what? These bastards won't give up so easily and it sure as shit won't be the last time I see them."

"We're going to keep you here. Not many people outside the family know about it, and it's well guarded. Once the heat dies down, we're going to move you to a safe house out in California. Only then will the heads of the family decide what to do with you."

I spun around in surprise, not believing my ears. "What? No, I cannot leave New York now. I ain't running from these pricks; no way!"

"Use your head, *bambina*. New York is not a place you want to be at the moment. Venom is going to come out of the woodwork, and they will tear the city to shreds looking for you. And once they find out the family was directly involved in freeing you, well, it's going to be a damn bloodbath, I can tell you that."

"And what about Peter and Richard? You just going to leave them there?" I was furious, the rage spilling out from me.

"I've already sent word and made arrangements to move them

to a safe house in a local theatre. We couldn't risk leaving them at the hospital—it was too obvious a target—but our contact in the theatre company assured me they will be well looked after there."

"You've got no idea what Venom is capable of. Everyone thought the Mafia ruled New York City, but it was a lie. They are the ones in charge. And there is nothing you can do to stop them except one thing . . ." My words trailed off, the tension palpable in the room.

"And what is that?" asked Vince skeptically, raising a bushy eyebrow in my direction.

"Me," I replied. "If it's true what they say about me, I'm the only chance you've got. We don't know how far Venom's influence stretches, but they've definitely got military and government contacts, and they will tear you to shreds without my help."

"And what makes you think you can make a difference? You're just a child."

"Fear. I saw it in Monroe's eyes; it was there no matter how hard he tried to hide it. He knew what I was capable of, even if I didn't. They made me the perfect weapon; it's time they experienced it for themselves."

"You would be willing to do that?" Vince asked, eyes wide in shock, an unusual feeling for the hardened Mafioso.

"I'll do it for my family, not for you. I don't give a shit about you or the Mafia. But to protect the ones I love, I'll rain hell on anyone that stands in my way."

"I'll have to clear this with the boss first. He won't be happy, but it appears we haven't got much of a choice in the matter."

Vince folded his fingers together and tapped them slowly on his forehead before looking up again. "If and only if I get approval, what would be your first plan of action?"

"Monroe. I've got a feeling he is still in New York City. I'm going to set fire to his world and see how many other rats I can lure out." My voice was soft and dangerous as I hissed the words.

"And if the boss says no? Then what?" asked Vince cautiously.

"Then every man on this farm is a corpse by tomorrow morning. Now be a good boy and get on the phone. I've had a long day and I want to get some shut-eye." Without saying anything more, I turned and headed up the steps, leaving the Mafioso stunned and his mouth hanging open.

The truth was that I wasn't going to turn in just yet.

I had one more thing to do for the evening. Choosing one of the upstairs rooms, I entered and locked the door behind me before sitting down on the overstuffed feather bed. I pulled the silver mask out from under my shirt, running my fingers over the cool metal. It hummed with eager anticipation at my touch. I must have sat there for what felt like hours, knowing that this was the point of no return.

Are you ready to do what is necessary? Can you truly live with yourself, Charlie? I had to. If I held back or hesitated for even a second, then everyone I ever loved would be dead. I had to do this, even if it destroyed me.

No going back.

The time had finally come to put the mask on. I slowly lifted it to my face, feeling the raw energy pulsating inside, the power unexplored seeping from it. It felt unearthly in my hands. The union of assassin and mask had finally come full circle; the bond was complete. I had taken a great step into the unknown, and nothing would ever be the same again.

"Let's see what you can do. Here we go."

A slew of numbers rushed past me, calculations too fast for the human mind to comprehend as a white haze surrounded me, my screams silenced as the room around me faded away. I was standing alone in a room of pure luminescence, the incandescent light so bright, so pure it blinded me for a moment, forcing me to shield my eyes. A metallic female voice echoed through the empty room, its tone cold and elegant as it spoke calmly to me.

"Welcome to Venom."

CHAPTER TWENTY-THREE

"Input password and name to proceed," the voice droned monotonously. "Failure to input correct password and name will result in immediate destruction of module and recipient."

I stood for a moment, entranced, as a green holographic keypad appeared before me, shimmering against the pure white background of the room.

Thinking deeply, my finger rested against the first number buzzing in and out of reality.

Could it be the same number I used back at Yankee Stadium? Was it really that easy? Hesitating again, I stopped and stepped back. *No, the security risk was simply too high to replicate the numbers. The mask must have had a higher security clearance, access specifically reserved for the higher-ups in the corporation. But what if there was a back door access meant as a fail-safe? One that only an agent could open?* Biting my lower lip, I stepped forward and tapped in a sequence. It was a shot in the dark, but I had to try it.

"Venom Zero Zero One. Charlotte." The machine hummed for a few seconds, analyzing my voice patterns before the keypad faded back into digital nothingness.

"Welcome, Agent Zero Zero One. I am at your service," the voice stated matter-of-factly, the room turning pitch-black as three computer screens materialized before my eyes.

"What are you?" I asked, still suspicious as to the machine's true purpose.

"I am Spider's Web version 2.0., the digital library and collective consciousness of the Venom Corporation. Please input commands to proceed."

"Give me options." The realization was clear to me that I was never meant to see the information stored inside this machine. That only in the most critical and dire of situations, with Venom's destruction imminent, would I become the safe keeper of all their insidious knowledge.

"One point zero. Current agent roster. Two point zero. Valkyrie sequence research. Three point zero. Restricted."

"Give me the names of all active agents," I replied, placing a palm on the computer screen.

"Two agents accounted for. Agent Venom Zero Zero One, last known location: New York City, USA. Venom Zero Zero Two, last known location: Severnaya Zemlya, Russia."

"I want the names." My voice had become ice cold and as hard as steel. There was someone like me out there in the world. Someone else that Venom had broken and twisted to their dark agenda. Someone like me who was alone and scared out of their mind.

"Agent Venom Zero Zero One: code name Charlotte Corday. Agent Venom Zero Zero Two: code name Lyudmila Pavlichenko.

Real names erased as per instruction of management."

I should have been furious, but a numbness settled over me. I still wasn't any nearer to knowing my true birth name. Still only a digital string of zeroes and ones, nothing more than that.

"Give me information on Agent Venom Zero Zero Two." I had to know more about this mysterious stranger, my counterpoint who was running free out there.

"Data erased. No image or any further information available." Someone had been in here long before me and made sure there was no trace back to them. I didn't know if she was under control of the corporation or if she was even still alive at this moment in time. Lyudmila remained an enigma to me.

"And Victor La Salle?"

"Project 45747998: location unknown, project has passed date of service and is scheduled for destruction—18 November 1971. No further information available."

Venom was going to put him down like a sick dog, and yet he came running back to them, hoping to win their approval one last time. Did he really expect mercy from them when they treated him like a laboratory experiment? Venom would never dare leave him alive, even if he had only the slightest fraction of training compared to me. He simply knew too much to be spared. *You were free, Victor. Why couldn't you just run away and never look back?* I thought glumly to myself, looking back at the computer screens. Even though I had barely known Victor and all he had wanted to do was kill me, in some way he felt like a brother to me.

"Any more information?" I asked, gathering my thoughts again.

"No further files on agents available. Data erased per order of management. Would you like to continue using my database Agent Zero Zero One?"

"Show me folder two point zero." There was no stopping now. I had to go further down the well, deeper into the darkness. *Fear is not an option now. You've got to be brave. Charlie, no matter what you see.*

"Access restricted to management level and agents with fail-safe designation. Do you want me to proceed?" the computer carried on, its words crisp and precise.

"Yes, I want to know everything."

"Accessing files."

What I saw next left me stunned and amazed.

Images of war flickered across the screens, of incredible pain and bloodshed, but one theme immediately stood out for me. In every battle, a female was involved, leading the charge from the front.

"Welcome to the Valkyrie sequence project," a voiceover stated as I looked on in awe, seeing Joan of Arc lay into the English at the Siege of Orléans, her sword scarlet red with blood as men fell at her feet by the score. "Research started in 1951, when a joint American and British science team came together to find the genetic marker that made us resilient as human beings. The hope was to isolate this gene so that we could then use it to improve soldiers on the various battlefields around the world, make them stronger with greater endurance to sustain them." The voice carried on while Boudicca, queen of the Iceni, charged across the green fields of England, turning a terrified Roman legion to ashes.

"The big breakthrough came five years later when we discovered that the resilience gene was considerably stronger in females than in males. We tested hundreds of female and male orphans taken from all over the world, and with each one, our research became stronger, our theories more proven."

Shaking my head in wonder, I saw Tomoe Gozen, the last onna-bugeisha (female samurai) rain hell down on her enemies, her feet swift, her bow a sweeping arc. She was beautiful and fearless, not yielding so much as an inch to any man. With her war cry still ringing in my ears, I focused back on the voiceover as it carried on unabated.

"Our hypothesis became clear through our intense studies in that if the resilience gene was already strong in a normal female, then how much more pronounced could it be in the great female warriors of lore? We sent out scores of archaeologists and retrieval agents all over the world to bring back DNA of these matriarchal goliaths of history, be it a bone, a lock of hair or a fingernail. At great expense, we gathered these priceless treasures, buying, stealing, even murdering when we had to, all for the greater good of humanity. From the farthest reaches of planet Earth they arrived at our laboratories in New York City. We gathered samples beyond human belief. Boudicca, Lozen, Cleopatra, Anne Bonny and Mary Read, Catherine of Aragorn, and many more—they all contributed to the project in one way or another.

"It took us ten long and grueling years to finally isolate the gene and stabilize it, but it wasn't enough for the governments of the day. They didn't just want a soldier that could last longer on the battlefield; the demand was for the perfect killer. They yearned for a killing machine, capable of destroying any human being at their call. The science had become twisted, and many of us left the project. In the late 1960s, Venom was established as a covert science division, funded by various world governments. They took the initial idea of harnessing warrior genes but spliced it with the most notorious female killers of history: Jael of the Kenites, Khioniya Guseva, and Brigitte Mohnhaupt among others; they were all added and incorporated into the gene sequence. The science worked, and we had finally captured the essence of the perfect assassin. Now we just needed the perfect test subject."

I looked on in horror as the once proud warriors of history faded away and were replaced by stone-cold killers, their hands dripping with blood. I couldn't pretend that their victims were innocent, but even I was shocked at the brutal images flashing before my eyes. The carnage and anarchy was beyond belief.

How could any organization be so fundamentally sick and twisted? I thought, the bile pushing up in my throat.

"Venom took hundreds of young girls from all over the globe, looking for those special individuals in whom the assassin DNA could be fused with their own. We left scores of bodies in our wake, but for the sake of appeasing our governments, we carried on with our experiments. Our final tally of assassins came down to ten girls, but eight had to be put down due to new government pressure. In the end, only you and Lyudmila survived, whisked away by the director for safekeeping. The hope was that with a change of government and time, the research of Venom would be seen in a more favorable light by those in charge. The future of Venom lies in your hands now, a future of control where extremists and fanatics can be put down in an instant. You are the perfect assassin; you are Venom, Charlotte Corday. End file."

I stood silently with cold revulsion pumping through my blood as the images finally faded away and the screens became blank again. *Is this what I really am? A soulless scalpel in the hands of the faceless overlords ruling this world?* I was no killer, but inside I knew the terrible truth: it was already decided for me. The genetics of thousands of years of bloodshed and mayhem was part of who I was today. I turned and vomited in the corner, my knees buckling as I held my stomach in agony. Wiping the acid taste from my mouth, I looked back at the blank screens mocking me from afar.

Why don't you just run, Charlie? Run and never look back. And then what? Did I really expect Venom and the monsters running it to just sit back with their arms crossed and let me go? To just give up on their perfect weapon after spending millions of dollars and decades in research? There was no fucking way they would do that. And what about Lyudmila? If she was still alive, they would hunt her down and pull every fiber from her body to get at the genetic code. As much as it hurt and tore me apart from the inside, I couldn't allow them to do that. I was the only one capable of stopping them.

"One folder left. Would you like to access it?" the computer asked, her voice emotionless, uncaring to the immense inner torment I was experiencing. I knew I had to carry on; there was no going back for me now.

"Yes," I replied, eyes lowered to the floor, not knowing how much more of this I could take.

"Folder only to be opened in case of imminent corporation destruction. Sensitive materials and information contained inside, access not advised. Would you like to return to the main screen Agent Zero Zero One?"

"No. I want to know what's inside." *No hesitation, Charlie. Don't look back.*

"Access granted. Warning . . . warning . . . System override enabled. Management protocols enacted." The machine beeped shrilly, lights flashing on and off in a chaotic jumbled mess of electronics before fading away into nothingness. In the blink of an eye, the room had changed from darkest black to an elegantly appointed and stylish office overlooking a crisp blue lake on a beautiful sunny morning.

"What are you doing, Charlotte?" a voice asked calmly behind me as I spun around in surprise. A holographic projection of a man was standing by a shelf of books, paging through a nondescript novel in a calculated and restrained manner, not looking up at me. He must have been in his late forties, perhaps early fifties, with silver and grey hair combed back over his ears. He was broad shouldered, like someone who was used to working out his entire life, his suit tailored, the grey material accentuating every muscle and fiber of his six-foot-four, toned body perfectly. I couldn't help but notice his hands, smooth and callus-free— the hands of a man not used to manual labor and taking orders. And then I saw the gold Venom insignia ring on his right finger, a symbol of hatred, of everything that I had come to loathe in life.

"Who are you?" I asked, my anger barely contained.

He closed his book, straightened his cuffs perfectly level, and then looked up at me with deep hazel-brown eyes. A look that pierced right into my very soul.

"Who am I? I am your father, Charlotte."

CHAPTER TWENTY-FOUR

"I have no father," I seethed as the figure casually poured himself a snifter of single malt whiskey.

"Well, not in a biological way, but in a conceptual sense, well yes." He swirled the brown liquid around, watching it cascade around the glass before carefully placing it to his lips.

"You're the sick bastard behind all this." I suddenly lunged at the man and collided hard with the wall. Just a hologram, a false illusion. *Stupid girl,* I thought to myself, slowly getting up from the ground, rubbing the welt that had formed on my shoulder. The man smirked, strolling over to an overstuffed executive chair behind the table before settling in.

"Oh, Charlotte, such fire and passion. You were always the strongest. If you could only see the truth I'm offering you."

"And what truth is that?" I said sarcastically, stalling for time. I had to figure out where this asshole was broadcasting from before I could put an end to him.

"The truth is whatever we say it is. Where we control the narrative of the modern-day world, not the bureaucrats and politicians anymore. Can you just imagine it?" He closed his eyes and leaned back in his chair, savoring the moment.

"All I can imagine is me kicking your ass." I dropped feisty words like bombs all around him while I studied his every move, every subtle play of his body. I wanted to breathe in my enemy, take over every part of his soul before destroying him.

"Leave the juvenile rage to someone who scares more easily than I. But you still haven't answered my question, Charlotte. What are you doing here?" His voice dripped with lavender oil and sweet poison.

"I already know everything about your messed-up organization, and when I'm done, I'm leaving it in a pile of blood and ashes. Hold me to that promise."

"My dearest child." He looked down from the ceiling, eyes cold and merciless as a winter's storm. "We both know that is not the truth. You came here looking for yourself."

"What?"

"Little Charlotte got a taste of pure power, felt the rush when she took a life at the museum, and now she wants more. Sniffing around like a vulture after scraps; so pathetic."

"Fuck you." *Don't let him lead you in, Charlie.* But I could not help myself; the monster was taking me ever deeper into the darkness.

"Hehehe." He laughed softly more to himself than anybody else before continuing. "The thing is, my child, you don't have to be satisfied with scraps. Not with what I'm offering you."

"And what is that?" My eyes narrowed as he stood up and looked out over the crystal-clear lake below.

"Everything. I want to give you Venom." He said it so

casually, as if it was something ordinary. Not believing what I had just heard, my jaw hung open in shock.

"You have to be joking. There is no way in hell I would ever do it," I finally managed to splutter.

"I would never reduce something so pure and powerful to a mere farce; there is too much value in what we do. No, it's simple, Charlotte. You are to take over the running of Venom at my passing. The immense power, the unimaginable control can all be yours. You just have to do one little thing."

"And what is that?"

"Just give up. That's all I ask. Once you surrender to us, you will be taken to one of our facilities where your DNA will be extracted and studied by our scientists. Your life will be spared, of course, and then you will take your rightful place by my side, to learn, to live, and to finally one day rule the empire I created." He finally turned around and I could see his cruel visage, the cool madness etched into his face.

"You're sick, and you are out of your damned mind," I hissed, the anger bubbling under my skin.

"Just imagine it, Charlotte, a world free of fanatics and the ideologically small content. Can you see it? The moment they show their faces, ready to maim and destroy our way of life, you and your sisters will be there to send them back to whatever god they wish. Isn't it just the most beautiful of visions? Can you see it my child?"

"And what gives you the right and the power to decide who lives and dies?" I had noticed something about the office, but I just couldn't put my finger on it yet. I had to keep him talking while I figured it out.

"It's the natural selection of predators over sheep, simple as that. These fools that think they run the world; they could never truly handle or understand this gift to humanity I created. And soon their time will be up and we will push them, screaming, to the rocks below. A new age of control and order is dawning where Venom becomes sentient. And right at the bleeding spear tip of humanity will be you and your sisters. It will be the zenith of our species." He was slightly hyperventilating, trying his best to hide it while he combed back an oily lock of black hair from his well-tanned face.

"And Victor? Where does he fit in with your so-called glorious plan?" I asked, stringing him along, playing for time. *There it is again; I'm sure of it now.* The thought flashed through my head but I kept my composure beatific, not giving anything away to the man.

"Ah, Victor. He was one of the first, a flawed test subject before we knew any better. How could we have known that the historical DNA would only work on female subjects? I wanted to give my boy a chance at greatness, but he became my greatest failing."

"Your boy?" I could not hide the shock in my voice when I realized he was not speaking figuratively. He had subjected his own flesh and blood to this hideous experiment.

"My first son from my second wife. He was dying from cancer, and I took a shot at bonding the warrior DNA to his own. Though it sent his cancer into remission, the DNA rejected him and left his mind shattered and fragmented. I had made the call to terminate my boy's life before he made his unfortunate escape from our New York facility. Victor was never supposed to live, not in this perfect new world. How could he? A pitiful slug amongst the roses."

"You're a soulless monster, but you haven't managed to kill him yet. That must chap your hide every day that he still breathes." *Keep him talking. You have to be sure. Can't make a mistake now.* The room flickered for a split second, quicker than the human eye could even register, but in that instant I knew my hunch was correct.

"He won't matter for long. Once I have you back in the fold and your DNA secured, I will simply send you after him and terminate his life. Even at ten percent, you are his superior in every way possible."

"Ten percent? What do you mean?" *Almost there, Charlie. Just a little bit further now.*

"I might as well tell you, seeing as it will be revealed to you soon, anyway." I could see the overconfident smile on his face as he ran a perfectly manicured finger over the rim of the now-empty whiskey glass.

"We realized early on in our research and after many unfortunate fatalities that the human body simply cannot handle the full extent of the warrior DNA. The original test subjects barely lasted a few minutes before their bodies shut down, crumpled up and twisted like a piece of worthless newspaper. They did not die pleasantly, but their contribution to the science was invaluable. So it was decided to only fuse ten percent of the DNA to your own, and for the first time, it worked. You never needed anything more than the tiniest sliver of this genetic nuclear bomb we held in our hands."

Got you. I started smiling, taking immense pleasure in seeing the sudden discomfort and confusion on the man's face.

"And what is so funny?" He stood up from the edge of his desk, straightening his shoulders and peering at me curiously.

"You are. When I first saw you, there was something off about you but I just couldn't place my finger on it. A brilliant scientist who looks like a male model; that's a stretch even for me, but okay, I'll bite. Then the room started flickering, faster than any human could ever sense it. You didn't think I would notice, but I did. I saw the outline, the bare bones that this fake image was built on. Then came the final bit of evidence I needed—why would there be a heavily secured file on the mainframe just to sooth your and my egos? It just didn't make sense, and then it finally dawned on me what you were hiding." I walked past the hologram, feeling the man's eyes sear into the back of my neck.

"What are you doing?" he hissed, all pretenses of civility suddenly gone. "I said what you doing, Charlotte?"

"This." I stepped up to the large glass pane at the edge of the office, turned, and faced him before spreading my arms wide. With a smile, I stepped back and fell backwards into nothingness. It was like a static bomb had exploded around me, the office and the gaping man from the far window swirling away into a chiaroscuroric jumble of greys and blacks. With a deep gulp of air, I was back in the black room, but things had changed. A crumpled-up figure in an old lab coat lay in a pile to the side and in front of me, and a glowing green box stood on a podium. Tantalizing, like it was calling my name louder with each passing second.

"You bitch . . ." I recognized the voice. It was the man from the office, but now I saw his true form: an old and withered shell of a man. He was a pathetic figure now that his cloak of smoke and ashes had dissipated into nothingness. "You could have had it all," he croaked, getting unsteadily to his feet and looking at me with pure hatred in his eyes. "An empire and the fate of billions at your fingertips, your every whim their command and you threw it away for what? A life lived in the gutters, between the scum and the rats? You are a fool, Charlotte." I ignored his tepid ramblings and focused on the box in front of me.

"What are you doing?" A thin trickle of blood ran down the side of his mouth as he watched with cold fascination as I opened the box, my face bathed in green light. "It's going to destroy you and everything I had worked so hard for."

I ran my hand over the glass cylinder, and I could feel the power bubbling inside. The warrior DNA coursed and thrashed inside, waiting, aching to be released.

"No human, nobody can handle it all. Do you hear me, Charlotte? Nobody!" he shouted, his tumultuous words breaking over me like a wave on rocks.

For a moment everything became quiet in me. I had entered the eye of the hurricane as I looked at him with a mixture of revulsion but also pity. He had given up his life and all those dear to him, all for the sake of this mad dream and untold amounts of power.

I was about to take everything away from him. "In case you haven't noticed, I was never normal." With a last look of resignation, I lifted up the cylinder and let it go. It fell as if in slow motion, fragmenting into a shower of crystalline shards.

Aghast, I stood as the images of a thousand warriors danced around me, some serene and at peace, others baying for war and blood. One by one they entered me, rushing inside as I held on for dear life, the stitches of my body straining and threatening to snap at any moment. The voices of a thousand zealots screamed with me, forcing me to my knees.

Give up, Charlie. You cannot do this . . . Just give up. You're not strong enough . . . the power . . . too much . . . have to let . . . go. My overwhelmed mind begged and pleaded with me to surrender, told me that I had reached my absolute breaking point, there was no going further. Please, no more.

No! Another, deeper voice rose up inside of me. It was the roar, the voice of a legion of women throughout history who were tired of being ridiculed, marginalized, and made fun of. Who had simply had enough. *Get up, Charlotte . . . Fight . . . fight for what is yours. Take it, take it all.*

I fought the power, inch for bloody inch, as I rose to my feet, veins arching, blood pumping a river of resolute pain through my body. I wrestled the demon to the ground, finally stomping my foot down and crushing its larynx under my boot. Finally, I stood tall, flexing my hands and feeling the power become one with me. The chanting echoes of the warriors faded away, but I knew we were now united. I carried their spirits with me.

Looking at the shocked visage of the man, I walked over and grabbed him by the collar.

"Impossible . . . It's impossible," he mumbled in disbelief.

"I'm going to burn your world to the ground, and you are

going to watch as I take it down brick by damn brick."

The man laughed softly, ruefully, as he looked at me with cold dead eyes. "You've signed your own death warrant. Even if we don't kill you, your body could never handle all the power. Eventually, it will consume you and tear your body apart. You're dead, Charlotte, and there is nothing you can do about it." He laughed hysterically before crumbling into grey ash.

Just another computer program. But I knew now who the architect of my misery was and how to stop him. The power was in me, and it felt damn good. Nothing would stand in my way anymore. I was in control.

"End program and exit," I said to the mainframe, and instantly I was back in the farmhouse bedroom.

The silver mask was in my hand but it felt different this time, less agitated and more settled and purposeful.

Lying back on the bed, I stared up at the ceiling and knew my story was only beginning now.

The hunt was renewed and the night belonged to me.

This is going to be fun.

CHAPTER TWENTY-FIVE

A heartbeat.

A pulse beating to a rhythm. Metronomic in consistency, never changing, never stopping. I could feel the city's pulse around me, frenetic energy like an unstoppable train in motion. Millions of voices, feelings, emotions . . . cascading, dancing through my mind; they were all inside me. I could reach out and touch every tiny ball of energy running around below me, hold their fate in my hands, the choice mine when to crush it, end their dreams at my slightest whim. The power was beautiful, and it was mine to control.

* * * * *

Midtown. New York City

I stood upon a windswept high-rise, listening to the fractured whispers of my city. She was in pain, chaos and anarchy etched into her voice. I could take it all away from her, relieve the symptoms, but first I had to remove the cancer, cut it from her belly. Soon it would be all over, the pain silenced. I closed my eyes and listened again, letting the power of the warrior inside guide me. There were no sounds, no screaming of voices inside my head, just the one solitary heartbeat I searched for.

Monroe.

I could taste the anxiety in him, feel the paranoia as he moved about the city. Cautious but calm, not expecting to be hunted; he must have thought I would be long gone by now. I mean, who would be mad enough to return to the raging storm that was New York City?

Only you, Charlie Only you.

Calmly leaping from ledge to ledge, a L96A1 sniper rifle in hand, I remembered the words of Vince just a few nights ago back at the farmhouse.

"*Mio Dio,* you have kicked over a hornet's nest, *bambina.* I got reports coming in from all over the city of sightings of these Venom *bastardos,* some even opening fire on members of the family. No fatalities, thank God, but I have men down and injured. There is even talk of going to the mattresses of all things," he said anxiously, squelching another spent cigarette into an already full ashtray.

"So, what you going to do?" I asked calmly, sitting cross-legged on an old wingback chair in the main dining room.

"We got to get the situation un-fucked, and quickly, That's what we're going to do. I can tell you, the boss is pissed, to put it very lightly, and he was not impressed to hear of your intentions to go back into the city. It took some very careful talking to convince him."

"He didn't have much of a choice, did he?" I laughed softly, privately to myself, feeling the humming of the mask inside my coat. I didn't want to let it out of my sight, not even for a moment, the feeling always there that the mask still had not revealed all its secrets. It was too precious to let fall into anyone else's hands.

"Incredible, but yes, he realized that the only way to stop Venom was to unleash their most powerful weapon back on them. But do not overestimate your value, Charlotte." He sat forward in his chair, cigarette hanging limply from an unshaven, stubbly face. "We won't hesitate to put you down if you become a liability, understand? There is no place for a rogue element in this dangerous game we play, and if you go beyond the family's control, we will end you without a second thought. Are we clear, *bambina?*"

"Just stay out of my way and let me work," I replied, sitting back and closing my eyes in thought, my words tinged in deepest ice.

Back to present day, I refocused my attention on the prey below. The old Charlie would have gone rushing in, overeager to take down the target no matter how messy or bloody it got. But I was calmer now, more focused and at peace with what I had to do. The hunt was almost serene in its cold and calculated brutality. It felt as if I had been doing it for hundreds of years.

I started stalking Monroe barely a day after I arrived back in New York City. He wasn't difficult to find, not with the resources of the Mafia at my disposal. As soon as I had changed my hair color from black to red and acquired another pistol from one of Richard's hidden stashes around the city, the hunt began.

Nice and steady, Charlie. Take your time. I was always a step behind him, constantly there wherever he went in the city. I mean, who of us really pays attention to the people around us? The person delivering the morning newspaper, the one that serves your coffee or drives you around. Have you ever truly looked? I was so close to him, watching his hand tighten around his coffee mug as I poured the thick black liquid in. It would have been so easy to kill him right there. Slash his throat and watch him bleed out on the diner's table, the blood mingling with the eggs over easy. I would have been gone before the waitress had time to scream.

What's come over you, Charlie? This is not you; get a grip, I thought to myself as I sheathed the silver butter knife up my sleeve and calmly walked out of the diner.

But it was me. I had the combined DNA of hundreds of years of bloodshed and slaughter in me and, for the first time, I could not deny that it felt good. I was dancing on the razor's edge, and with every moment that passed, the feeling of ultimate control grew stronger in me.

Are you really in control, Charlie? Really? I silenced the nagging voice in my head and waited patiently outside for Monroe to finish his breakfast, toying with him like a cat plays with its food. The rush of feeling his heart beating wildly when he thought he was being followed but seeing nothing behind him.

That's it . . . keep going. I let the string out before pulling him back gently, time and again. But he was smart and cautious, never making contact with any other Venom associate. His routine was purposefully mundane so as not to attract any attention. But he had mine, and now I knew his every step, every thought before he even made it. All I had to do was press my foot down hard on his throat and watch the rat scurry for cover.

So very easy.

I was back in the present, the wind carrying on unabated through my red hair, a 7.62x51mm NATO cartridge spinning in my fingers as I looked calmly down at Monroe's apartment below. Ground floor access for easy escape, typical New York brownstone, nothing to draw attention.

Predictable. I watched with casual interest as he approached up the street, *New York Times* under his arm. Always at the exact time and always using the exact route. I even knew the exact layout of his apartment; breaking in was child's play for me. Monroe wouldn't have the balls to keep a weapon inside. No, I just wanted to move his telephone a few meters, right in front of the window.

He fumbled for his keys, looking around cautiously before entering the brownstone apartment. It was 17:00 exactly as I smiled and loaded the cartridge into the sniper rifle, taking careful aim down the scope. The phone rang shrilly in his apartment, making the normally taciturn agent jump as he spun around.

Good to have a union member in the phone company.

I knew exactly what he was hearing at that very moment.

"Look up." His eyes were wide in shock as I pulled the trigger and watched the phone disintegrate in his hand, the shrapnel burying deep into his flesh. Even from the roof of the high-rise, I could hear his screams of agony. A dark part of me took intense pleasure from his suffering.

This is not you, Charlie. This is not you. Wiping the rifle down and dropping it down a ventilation shaft, I calmly walked down the fire escape and waited for Monroe to make his escape from the apartment.

Come on, little rat, make a break and run for it. I pulled a bag from a nearby dumpster in the alley, slipping the brown overcoat over my shoulders and placing a long blonde wig over my red hair. The wailing of incoming police sirens didn't faze me; they would simply be chasing shadows. All I was focused on was the man running from his apartment, bloody hand wrapped in white bandages. All semblances of caution and control were gone as he shouldered his way through the crowds outside. It was so easy to follow his trail, Monroe's heart threatening to explode in his chest, the sweet smell of adrenaline filling the air. He could run as far as he wanted to; it didn't matter anymore.

I had caught the scent of my prey.

A Yellow Cab roared away as he tried to climb in, the driver seeing the bloody appendage hanging by his side. It was beautiful to feel the pheromones of fear and panic rushing from Monroe, knowing he could never escape me. All the while herding him deeper into my trap. Down the alley ways and side streets of New York, I shepherded the rat, carefully boxing him in. It was perfectly planned, every stolen car, every stack of crates placed beforehand with a cold and calculated mind.

"Monroe . . . Monroe . . . Monroe," I chanted down the deserted alleyway, toying with my prey. There was no place to run.

Finally, I caught up with him at the end of a closed-off alley.

Desperately, he clawed at the chain-link fence but to no avail as he turned around and saw the dark etching of my silhouette in front of him. Falling to his knees, he begged pitifully as I walked closer, Glock steady in my hand.

"Mercy, please. I beg of you, mercy!" Monroe pleaded. The wind sent shards of discarded paper cartwheeling down the alleyway as I looked at him with hatred flashing in my eyes.

"Mercy? You want mercy from me when you destroyed my whole life?" The first shot rang out, eviscerating his left knee. "Tried to kill the ones I love?" The next shot made sure he would never use his right knee again. I picked the bloody, pathetic remnants of Agent Monroe up by his throat, my fingers driving deep into his quivering flesh. For the first time, I saw fear in his eyes, and I loved it.

"And now you are going to talk," I hissed as I slowly, methodically cut off his oxygen supply till he became limp and passed out before me. Calmly standing up and wiping the blood from my hands, I opened a nearby alley door and dragged the comatose body inside. It was an old storage room, empty save for a simple wooden chair in the middle. Tying him securely to the chair, I stepped back and nodded appreciatively at my handiwork.

"See you soon," I whispered before walking out and closing the door behind me. There was one thing I had to do before I could focus my full attention on him.

Just one thing.

Two hours later. Broadway. Winter Garden Theatre.

Slowly, I entered the theatre, looking around and pulling my collar up tightly. The place was deserted, and all the performers had gone home for the evening. All save for two standing alone in front of the stage. Walking past the red velvet seats, I took a deep breath, a gentle smile forming on my face.

"Richard, Peter?" I said, fighting to hold back the tears. They spun around and embraced me tightly, the shock and relief palpable on their faces. We must have stood there for a good ten minutes, not saying anything, just sobbing our eyes out.

There in that little theatre, I had found my family again.

CHAPTER TWENTY-SIX

I could not find the words, the relief at finding my godparents again overwhelming me. I didn't care who saw us there, be it Venom or the Mafia or who the hell ever; at that perfect moment it just didn't matter. The world stopped as we looked at each with tears running down our faces. I was finally home again.

The storage room was cold and sterile. I wondered to myself when last a human being was inside here, to set foot on the unforgiving cement inside. It was just me and him now, his face illuminated by the yellow flickering bulb swinging above his head. Head slumped low, blood flowing from shattered knees as I grabbed his matted blond hair and pulled his head back violently. "You are going to tell me everything I want to know, one way or another."

"Fuck you," he spat, blood pirouetting down his face, graceful in their morbid and silent tragedy.

"I'm sorry . . . I'm so sorry. I should never have left you. Sorry . . ." I mumbled as Peter and Richard stepped back and looked at me with the kindest of eyes, eyes which I did not deserve.

"It's okay, dear; you can tell us all about it over supper. The theatre cook has some leftovers kept warm for us. The lovely soul insisted on cooking for us while Peter recovers from his accident. Thank God." He whispered that last part to me as I turned my head and snickered.

"What was that?" Peter replied, momentarily distracted by something onstage.

"Nothing, dahling. Come along now."

His screams, why couldn't I hear his screams? The thoughts kept coming to me as I cut Monroe's veins open, the dark red blood, sticky, splashing on my skin as I tore him further open inch by inch. Why did I want him to scream? What dark and demented passenger inside me yearned to hear his banshee like howling? To savor the feeling when his will finally broke and he gave in to me?

"Where is the Venom headquarters in New York City?" *I asked quietly and calmly, driving the knife deeper into his sweat-stained skin.*

"Fuck . . . you." *His words were incoherent and fading fast. Had to keep him alive for a little while longer.*

It was a simple meal, roast chicken left over from yesterday's show, served with a whole potato and a salad. It didn't need to be anything more than that; I was content and happy where I was. Not realizing how hungry I was, I tucked in without much ceremony. It had been days since I last had a proper meal; I couldn't even remember when. As I shoved the food in my mouth, the others sat back and watched me intently with smiles on their faces. When I finally stopped, I looked up sheepishly at them, blushing beet red.

Grimacing in pain, Peter leant over and took my hand in his.

"Want to tell us what's going on, dear?" he asked with compassion in his eyes.

I pushed my food around on my plate, looking down at the ground before stating softly, "I'm in with wrong crowd and I don't know how to get out."

Where was my voice of reason? The subconscious part of me that was always there for me, was she finally dead? I couldn't help but think that I lost something of me that night at the farm. Was my humanity, a soul perhaps, or maybe just that scared little girl that was too afraid to do what needed to be done. I slammed the alligator clips into his veins, fastening them tightly on shivering bone. "The Venom headquarters in New York City. Tell me." My words were cruel and merciless as Monroe twisted his head to the side, fear evident for the first time in his eyes.

"Fuck you." His conviction diminishing, clinging on by its last precious strands as I flipped the power switch and watched the world change from black to white.

"We will always be here for you, dahling." Richard held my shoulder tightly, his grip strong and comforting. This was wrong, I should never have involved them, but who else could I possibly turn to? There was no one else out there for me. A noise made me spin around, bread knife in hand. It was nothing, just a stagehand walking by. Destroying whoever came before me was my first instinct now. And in that tragically poignant moment, I finally cracked. The knife dropped to the floor below as I held my hands up to my face, shaking and crying with agony, clutching my head. Just make it stop, just make it stop.

"New York Power, I could leave this on for days. Nobody can hear you scream, and nobody can smell your burning corpse. You will die alone, your ashes swept up in a black bag and thrown into

some forgotten dumpster out there. Who will mourn you, Christopher Monroe? Venom? You are just another replaceable pawn to them; there are thousands of you out there. Just give me the location of the headquarters and I will stop. Simple as that," I purred, waiting for his inevitable answer.

"Fuc—" He never got a chance to finish his sentence as I ripped the crocodile clamps from his arms and smashed them into his mouth, hearing the satisfying snap of breaking teeth. The clamps sunk deep into his red, inflamed tongue, his screams for mercy snuffed out.

"We got you, dear; we got you, dear." My godparents wrapped their arms around me as I sat hunched over on the ground, trembling violently. I felt Richard look up to Peter, the worry clearly evident in him.

"We've got to get her out of here; whatever is going on, she cannot stay in New York City," he said, never letting go of me for even an instant.

"But where?" asked Peter, stroking his long angular chin. "We could send her to one of our weapons contacts across country, but they are constantly watched, so no, that simply won't do."

"What about Cousin Mickey?"

"Dear Lord, you must be mad. There is no way that will work. That will mean sending her to . . ." Peter stood aghast, not believing the words coming from Richard's mouth.

"Yes, but anything is better than this mad house. We have no choice."

My inner sadist finally turned off the power and watched the convulsing body strapped to the chair in front of me finally come to rest. Somehow, I knew exactly when to stop, just before he crossed over into death's realm. Slowly, I released the crocodile clamp from his tongue, seeing his bloody body torn apart by the force of the current. He was bleeding profusely, but he had to stay alive just for a few more seconds.

One more act to go.

"Venom. Now." My words bade no resistance or pity.

"Please . . . please, I can't. They will kill . . . everyone I . . . love." He pleaded.

"They took everything you ever loved, stole your very soul. Why should you give them mercy, Charlie? They never showed you any, not for one second. Have you got the balls to do what is necessary?"

I reached into a bag behind me and pulled out a five-pound bag of salt. Slowly tearing open the plastic, eyes emotionless, I poured it out over his head and stepped back. Blood bubbling under the onslaught of the salt, skin and veins tearing back in beautifully realized agony. He cried and screamed like a child, body convulsing violently as he tried in vain to escape his bonds. And then finally, he talked.

"Three fifty-five East . . . Fifty-Second . . . street. Now please . . . Please kill me." He begged like a pathetic scrub. I turned and walked away, looking over my shoulder at the pitiful sight.

"No."

"I have to go, I can't stay here. I'll be back later, promise." Looking at my godparents with tear-stained eyes, I ran from the theatre kitchen and out into the waiting night.

Don't look back, Charlie. Don't look back.

I had to find somewhere quiet, a place where I could just calm the voices inside my head, even if it was just for a short while.

Had to get away . . . had to get away. I wandered the streets of New York like a mad person, not knowing where I was going, stumbling between the painted whores and the night scum. I didn't care who saw me; it didn't matter to me anymore.

Make it stop . . . make it stop. I fell over a hot dog cart, soaking myself in dirty water and tomato sauce. Picking myself up, face blank and emotionless, the screams of the vendor drowned out as I wandered aimlessly on.

Then I saw him. Some godless dealer sprawled out in a dark alleyway, the dull glint of a freshly pulled needle in his hand. I beat him to death with my bare hands that night.

No remorse.

No regret.

With the needle stuck in my vein and the heroin pumping through my body, the voices finally quieted down and I could find peace again as I passed out against the alley wall, my body coated in the dealer's blood as he lay silently next to me.

Finally, I could rest . . . I could . . . rest.

CHAPTER TWENTY-SEVEN

Why can't they let me sleep? I sat up in the rubbish-strewn alley and pushed the blood-soaked body of the dealer away from me, empty eyes staring lifelessly into an unknown void. What was his name and why did it even matter to me? *Why can't I feel anything?* I felt no remorse at his violent passing; he was just another corpse standing in my way, another one that had to fall before I could reach another empty goal. A cold feeling came over me, and I knew that this street trash would not be the last to die at my hands; there would be plenty more to come. I would have to flow a river of blood to Venom's doorstep. It was the only way to stop this madness. The only way I could find peace again.

Body aching, I rose from the cold cement and looked around me. The walls of the derelict building were spinning, arching, threatening to collapse on me. *Have to get away . . . Have to find the headquarters.* Fumbling for the pistol in my inner coat, thankful that it was still there, I wiped the blood from my mouth and stumbled away from the cold and rigid corpse left behind. The sun had barely risen over the New York skyline, the late-night scum, the vampires that lurked in the razor-blade-filled corners of our collective darkest nightmares already running for cover before the golden rays of the morning. The Big Apple was stirring, but I did not care; my only goal was to reach 355 East Fifty-Second street before Venom could run like rats again. *Hurry, Charlie . . . Faster . . . Faster.* In my drug-induced state, I could feel the heartbeats of the people around me, the businessmen in their fancy suits, the cops with their snouts in a box of early morning doughnuts, the babysitter that just fucked someone's husband. A heaving mass of thundering hearts, beating loud . . . so loud, till I started screaming and clutching my ears in pain.

Run, Charlie, run!

Their faces morphing, melting, blood mixing with yellow fat as it ran down their faces, the demons gathering around me. Steel jaws, wicked claws . . They were coming for me . . . never stopping . . . never stopping. Fighting my way through the nightmares, the buildings grew arms—long, black, wispy arms thrashing violently at me from the darkness surrounding. More and more they came, marching legion line as the demons of the night stalked ever moving before them.

You cannot face them alone, Charlie. You have to run. Run and don't look back. Lowering my shoulder and breaking through the wall of darkness, I saw a carriage approaching through the gloom, fire breathing horses pulling it through the night. A pale skeleton dressed in a black cloak sat atop it as I pulled my pistol on the creature, hand trembling violently.

"Three fifty-five East Fifty-Second Street, now." What came over me to demand this of the creature I will never know. It must have been the heroin talking, but I did not care.

The overwhelming lust for vengeance drove me forward into the darkness. I had lost control and I just did not give a fuck anymore. There was only the next mission, the next goal, the next corpse. The skeleton laughed wickedly, head falling to the side, chattering away into the night as I got on board. The demon horses spat flames as they charged past ghostly forests and howling wolves, the wind rushing through my hair as I grimly held on, the driver whipping the horses into a furious frenzy, driving them ever faster, his laughter maniacal as he swept past fear-struck villagers.

It's just the heroin talking. Keep it together, Charlie. Just keep it together. My hallucinations became reality, the trip carrying me ever forth into the drug-fueled nightmares of my deepest subconsciousness. All the most intimate horrors of my mind played out before my eyes—every soul I destroyed, every life I took danced marionette-like next to the road, some hanging from gallows ropes, others crucified and staring blankly at me as we flew past.

And I laughed.

Madness took hold, overwhelming me as I threw my head back in delirium and howled with crazed laughter. Even the driver peered at me through hollow black eyes, unsure what to make of this pure insanity next to him. All those souls I had slaughtered, the wake of bodies left behind, they just did not matter to me, merely dominoes I could push over whenever I wanted to. I was going to add so many more to my collection of souls, and there was nothing they could do to stop me. The power of a thousand female warriors coursed through my blood, their DNA forged in steel and iron of millennia past, and it all belonged to me. It felt good to finally embrace my true power and purpose and leave that frightened little girl behind, my foot crushing her skull as I walked by. Never go back to being that pathetic child, unsure of her place in the world, too afraid to take what is rightfully hers. No, she died the moment I put on that mask and embraced the power of the Valkyrie.

No, Charlie, no. You've gone too far. Come back . . . Come back . . . The voice of reason pleaded in my mind, but I ignored her, pushing the conscience away.

Quietly, oh so quietly, it turned away from me and faded away into the misty gloom. I would not need it again, not where I was going. The horseman finally pulled up, shadow horses breathing heavy fire as they paced restlessly around. A dark building, many stories high and bathed in colors of grim, stood before me, and I knew my lonely road led straight to it.

No turning around; no going back. With one last glance at the skeletal horseman, I leapt off the carriage as he tipped his top hat at me before roaring off back into the stygian night, his presence only a memory left behind. Walking toward the forbidding structure looming over me, I became aware of two lines of figures standing to the side, bathed in unearthly green light.

They were me.

A thousand Charlottes from a thousand different lifetimes all stood looking quietly at me. There I was, the strung-out junkie that OD'd at fifteen, a forgotten corpse found on the streets of New York City. There I was, dressed in bridal white silk on the day of my marriage, happy and smiling. There I was, a mother, a gentle hand stroking over my swollen belly. There I was, the warrior with a smoking pistol, the one seeking redemption for the sins committed against her. There I was, the murderer with blood on her hands.

There I was.

One by one, the green visions of lives past and chances forgone faded away as I slowly walked by them. Were they missed opportunities or premonitions on the road forward? Did it really matter to me?

And then came the last vision, standing squarely in my way.

The avenger.

She held out two ethereal pistols to me, their sleek, black lines shimmering in the greyish gloom surrounding me. Exhaling slowly, I wrapped my hands around the bases of the weapons, feeling the heft in my hands. The choice was made, and there was no going back for me now. Nodding at the vision, I lifted the pistols high and walked past her. Pausing for a moment at the inlaid door, thick streams of blood running down the ingrained wood, I kicked it in and rushed into the unknown. I could feel myself letting go, giving over to the demonic crusader inside. Charlotte had finally lost control.

The twin pistols spat lead and fire, lighting up the melanoid darkness of the room as the monsters lurking in the corners fled for cover. It would be of no use; each and every one of these bastards was going to die today. I was going to send a loud and clear message to Venom, one that they dared not ignore. Slowly, methodically, I walked through the empty room, each shot aimed deadly true. Each shot down another monster that would never hurt another person ever again. They squealed and shouted as they tried to run from me, bullets ripping their backs to shreds and painting the walls in shades of scarlet. Some cajoled and begged for forgiveness, claws wrapped together in pathetic pleas for mercy.

Mercy? Why should you show them mercy when they never showed any to you? I executed another faceless monster at point-blank range, shards of gore and brain cascading through the air.

Kill.

Reload.

Kill.

The more blood I shed, the more ravenous the demon inside me became, its unquenchable thirst never sated. It screamed and thrashed away inside my soul, willing me on relentlessly for more anarchy, more destruction, more death. I had never felt this pure loss of control as the muzzle flashes lit up my face in the dark, giving myself over to the creature inside. There was always the voice of conscience in my head, the one that always brought me back from the brink and kept my sanity in check. But Charlie was gone. I had killed her off when I walked through that door, and she was never coming back.

More, Charlotte, more! The voice bayed as I unloaded two spent magazines, watching them clatter to the ground and fall away. I climbed under the faceless monsters and started beating them with the butt of a pistol, their pitiful screams soon turning to blood-gargled cries of death. But I did not stop, did not hesitate for even a moment as the scarlet gore ran down my face.

They took everything from you, Charlotte. They spat on your dreams. End them. End them now.

I could not be sure how long the massacre lasted. Ten minutes? Twenty minutes, perhaps? Time became irrelevant in the slaughterhouse of my design as I wailed furiously, helplessly into a pile of broken bodies. They were already long dead, bloodied marionettes flailing around each time my fists crashed into their lifeless skulls.

"Fuck you . . . Fuck you . . ." I choked the words from my body, barely whispering them as I hit them harder still, the taste of blood filling my mouth. And then slowly, I rose to my feet and looked around me. The heroin haze finally lifted and everything became clear again. There was no darkened room around me and no faceless monsters. Just daylight and an unthinkable scene that unfolded before my eyes.

With a cold, descending feeling of dread dawning on me, I realized what I had done. This was not Venom. It was just a normal office building with normal, everyday people going to work inside it.

Sinking to my knees, I lifted up the mutilated body of a young man, barely twenty if he was a day. His head hanging limply to the side as I started shaking in the sheer realization of my actions, looking at the bullet-ridden grey cubicle walls painted in swathes of dark red and brain matter. At least thirty corpses lay eerily still on the once light-blue carpets of the office, the sudden silence enveloping them all, the ring of gunshots and screams of the dying faded away. They never had a chance against me, some making it precariously close to the exit doors before I ripped their souls from their bodies.

How could you have trusted Monroe, you stupid little girl? It was almost an afterthought that the agent had lied to me with his last remaining action, sending me to the wrong address as a final fuck you. Aimlessly, I stumbled past corpse after corpse, stupidly hoping that maybe one had somehow survived. Like that would have made any difference to what I had done.

No survivors. My kill shots precise and deadly, leaving no one alive in the office. I wanted to scream bloody murder, bang my fists on the walls till the bones poked through and the blood ran over them, but there was nothing left inside me, just a hollow and shattered shell. It was the remnants of Charlotte Corday, destroyer of the innocent. A single pistol round rolled around in my pocket as I slowly took it out and turned it over in my fingers, looking at the cruel elegance of its design. Falling to my knees on the plush blue carpet between the scattered remains of the corpses around me, I placed the round in the still-smoking chamber of the pistol. I had nothing to live for, and I had become everything that I despised Venom for. Through my own hand, I had finally become their perfect weapon, the killer they always wanted. *They will never have me. No one will.* Closing my eyes, I placed the barrel of the pistol in my mouth, the hot metal leaving blisters on my lips as I pulled the trigger and waited for the end.

I'm sorry . . . No more pain, no more suffering.

Just my final moments of infinite regret.

But it never came. The relief of ending my existence was denied me as I opened my eyes and looked up. Vince was standing over me, hand on the pistol, blocking the hammer with a large meaty finger.

"*Santos Christos*, this is not the way, Charlotte," he said, trying desperately to hide the shock in his voice as he lifted me into his large arms and carried me out, a cacophony of police sirens bearing down on us.

"Let me go . . . let me go . . ." I mumbled incoherently into his shoulder, blood dripping from my red hair onto his clothing. But he would not listen to me. Why would he not listen to me?

"Quiet now, *bambina,* quiet." The massive Italian ran with me from the scene of the massacre, bursting out of the broken-down doors and into the light of early morning New York City. Out of the corner of my eye, I saw the car I had hijacked earlier, the driver slumped over dead at the wheel. Just another victim of my madness, of my bloodlust and ego.

I almost didn't feel it as Vince pushed me into the waiting car and roared off down the city streets, flashing red and blue lights exploding behind us. I could feel nothing, just a terrible sequence of words that kept repeating itself over and over in my mind like the repetition of a broken children's rhyme.

What have I done? What have I done? What have I . . . done?

CHAPTER TWENTY-EIGHT

The world was in silence around me. Maybe I didn't want to hear anything, wanted to block out the screams of pain echoing in my mind, to wish it all way. I saw Vince sitting upright next to me, fighting furiously with the wheel, leaning over and shouting at me periodically. His mouth moved in soundless angry patterns, face lit in shades of flashing blue and red as a swarm of NYPD vehicles careened after us. My expression remained emotionless as the black Lincoln Continental weaved through the New York traffic, shards of metal flying, cars crashing into each other behind us. I saw the faces of terrified pedestrians flashing by us, the horror etched into their souls. I could feel the terror inside them, sense the adrenaline pumping inside while they ducked and ran for cover. For a moment, I wondered if somehow they knew the people I had slaughtered mere moments ago. Were they someone's family, a friend, a fiancé, a lover? What would they say when they saw the bodies draped in white sheets being carried from the building? Was there anything left to say? I knew I would feel their souls dying inside, perhaps in minutes, an hour, or days, but there was no running or hiding from the sickening reality.

The reality that I had butchered those innocent people and there was nothing I could do about it. My anger and pride had led to this . . . God, why did Vince stop me from pulling the trigger? I was so damn close to ending it all. So damn close . . .

I looked slowly over at the big Mafioso as he grabbed my head and pushed it down to the floorboards, the rear window exploding in a shower of glass shards, bullets streaking tracer-like past us.

"*Get down!*" he shouted, leaning back and firing a brace of shots at the pursuing cop cars. It did little to deter them. They just kept on coming, never stopping, never hesitating or slowing down for even a moment. Up above, a news helicopter was circling, watching the drama unfold. It didn't take the vultures long to get wind of the breaking story, salivating at the prospect of further human misery. Maybe it was worth giving them what they wanted—a silent and violent end to it all.

"Let me out . . ." I said, calm as death.

"What?!" shouted Vince as he threw the car around a corner, wheels spinning and protesting violently as he fought to keep the Lincoln upright before sideswiping a hot dog stand, sending the hapless cart crashing through a shop front window.

"Let me out . . . I deserve this. Let them shoot me," I mumbled, the last vestiges of the heroin still in my system. Still couldn't focus . . . couldn't understand what was going on.

"Shut the hell up, Charlotte, and keep your damn head down! We are going to lose them in Brooklyn." An NYPD cruiser sped up next to us, the cop leaning out, waving his police issue piece at us, his shouting lost in the melee of traffic rushing by. Gritting his teeth, Vince slammed on the brakes, smoke pouring from the red-hot brakes as he watched with cold, remorseless eyes as the cruiser thundered head on into an oncoming taxi, a cascade of flying metal and sparks following the gruesome scene. Shifting up a gear, he willed the Lincoln forward, glancing over his shoulder at the incoming storm of black-and-white cop cars.

"Got to lose them . . . Where is it? Dammit, where is it?" he kept repeating to himself, never taking his eyes off the road as we slalomed between rows of cars, yellow sparks flying as metal scraped on metal. It was carnage on the streets, bent and twisted hunks of steel littering the roads as the Lincoln flew ever onwards, a sea of cop cars in close pursuit. It couldn't last, a spike strip or a roadblock bringing a sudden and violent end to our escape. Still in a haze, I fumbled for the door latch and watched it swing open. Leaning out, feeling the tar skim past my face . . . I was so close . . . Just had to let . . . go. I could already see myself standing up off the road, blood dripping from road-rashed skin, the cops surrounding me. My final act to empty my magazine into the air, screaming wordlessly as a hundred bullets tore me to shreds.

It was all I deserved. The death of Charlotte Corday. A sudden end to it all.

"What the fuck are you doing, *bambina*?" He lunged over, grabbing me by the collar and dragging me back inside the car, my head slamming into the brown leather seat as he struggled to regain control with one hand. Seething silently, he pushed the Town Car to its limits, smoke pouring from the battered and busted engine. And then, just I had feared, our luck finally ran out. A line of New York's finest were waiting for us in the distance, standing with shotguns in hand behind their cruisers. The entire Twenty-Seventh Street lay empty and deserted before us, not a soul in sight.

"Can't run anymore . . . Just let me go." But if Vince saw the look of fear in my face, he took no notice of it. He simply smiled, more to himself than anybody else, before grasping the gear lever tightly.

"Hold on." He slammed the Lincoln into first and charged down the empty street, the spent wheels on their tired last legs, but he willed them for one little bit more effort. It was a suicide run; it had to be. We would be slaughtered before we even got near the police picket line; he had to know that, surely. There was no way this was going to work.

Oh, what the hell. We all got to go sometime, right? I thought grimly to myself, digging my fingers deep into the fake leather seat, waiting for the inevitable to happen. No looking back. This was it; the moment I had yearned for had arrived.

Time to end this.

The car roared mightily, summoning up the last remaining energy it had from the V8 Ford Windsor engine underneath it. I could feel the wind rushing through the bullet-ridden body as the Lincoln picked up speed, pistons and valves screaming in tortured stress as Vince pushed it past its breaking point.

Five hundred yards. Four hundred yards. Three hundred yards.

Suddenly Vince threw the wheel to the left, the car bouncing over the curb, threatening to flip over at any moment; how he kept it upright was beyond me. Then I saw what he was aiming for.

"*No frickin' way.*"

The last thing I saw before darkness enveloped us was a sign flashing overhead—*Fort Hamilton Parkway*. We hit the subway steps with a screeching of metal finally resigned to its fate as the car fell to pieces on the rock-hard cement steps. The Lincoln buckled and swerved, a wheel breaking off and bouncing off into the dimly lit cavern below.

"Hold on!" Vince shouted as we crashed through the metal turnstiles, a shower of coins exploding into the air behind us as shocked onlookers dived for cover.

"Come on! Come on, damn you!" he ranted furiously, turning the car into an almost uncontrollable sideways skid. Axels snapping, steel tearing, a stationary subway train rushing ever closer, I closed my eyes and waited for the impact.

Closer . . . closer. And then by some miracle, the Lincoln started to slow down and came to a stop with a bump against the subway carriage. The Lincoln's lights flickered for the last time and faded away. I couldn't believe it, but we had survived the trip into madness.

"Hurry now, *bambina*, before they get here." Vince dragged me from the wrecked Town Car to the waiting train. The doors slid open and two men pulled us in.

"We almost thought you weren't going to make it, boss," rumbled the first one, a large bear of a man with oily black hair holding an AK47 in his hands.

"Just a slight delay. Tell Ernesto to get this thing moving

rapidamente. We need to get out of here before the entire fucking NYPD comes down on us. Now move." His orders were crisp and clear as a second, mouselike man got on to a two-way radio. Moments later, the subway train lurched forwards, iron wheels screaming in the shocked silence of the station. We could hear the wailing sounds of rapidly approaching cop cars and the hollers of police officers, but they were too late; we had made good our escape.

Vince only relaxed once we were well underway, the lights of the station fading away down the tunnel. Exhaling deeply, he grabbed my hand and dragged me down the passage to an empty carriage, wearily pushing open the metal door. Before I could gather myself, he slammed me against the wall, my body shuddering under the impact of the big Mafioso as he reached into my coat and pulled out the silver Venom mask.

"And now you are going to tell me exactly what the fuck is going on. I want to know every damn detail, and don't you dare hold back on me."

"I don't know what you are talking about. Get off me." I spat the words out as Vince snarled, slapping me hard in the face, leaving a stinging welt behind, blood dripping down my torn lip.

"I said don't you fucking dare lie to me, little girl!" His face was red with anger in the dimly lit subway carriage, fingers digging deep into my aching shoulder. For a moment, I wanted to resist him and fight back, but my body sagged, and for the first time I looked up, straight into his ice-blue eyes. There was no use lying to him anymore, no sense in hiding the truth.

Even though I despised the Mafia and everything they stood

for, at this moment they might be my only allies left as my world burnt around me. I had come to the end of the line with no going back, not with an entire city out for my blood. Venom, the NYPD, the Feds — I was now number one on their hit list, and I bet they were itching to take me down. It would have been so easy to simply walk out and give myself over to them, so very easy. Yet I couldn't answer the simple question of why I couldn't bring myself to do it.

I didn't know if it was the bloodlust of the warriors raging inside me that was satisfied for a while, but the storm was still, the dark clouds drifting off. For the first time, I truly felt tired, like I was running on empty and didn't have anything more to give.

Time to stop running, Charlotte. It was weird, but for once the voice in my head was not a charging call to battle but a soft, almost delicate voice of reason, healing my wounds after the carnage I had caused. Maybe there was still some hope left inside me, no matter how far away it seemed.

I made up my mind right there and then that I had to tell Vince the whole story, no matter how much it hurt. I had to get it all out, piece by damned piece, till it was done.

Do it, Charlotte. Do it.

CHAPTER TWENTY-NINE

"Venom," I began, picking my words very carefully. How did you explain something so completely crazy when you yourself didn't actually understand it? "There was something in that mask I took from them. Something that changed me inside."

"Bullshit." Vince fished a hand -rolled cigarette from his pocket and expertly lit it before flipping the lighter closed. "I don't believe you."

"I don't care what you believe. This thing changed me. I am faster, stronger, more capable than the most elite of soldiers. I've become the weapon they always wanted me to be."

"A soldier has control and restraint, but you, *bambina,* are totally out of control. Do you have any idea of the shitstorm that you have caused?"

"I can't help it!" I shouted, smashing my fist through a nearby window. A thin trickle of deep-red blood ran down my hand as I tried to cover it under my coat. "This monster inside me, it wants me to kill. The bloodlust, the hunger for more carnage . . . I . . . I can't stop it." Gritting my teeth, maybe to hide the shame in my eyes, I turned my head away from him.

"Christ. Is there any chance anybody else can get this . . . this virus you have?" Vince asked, eyes narrowing in apprehension as the subway shadows played over his face.

"It's not a damn virus. I don't know what it is. I just want it out of me, and no, I don't think anyone else can get it. I was the only one with access to the computer inside the mask." I sagged down on a bench, holding my head in my hands before looking up at Vince again. "How did you find me, anyway?"

"It wasn't difficult, not with the chaos you caused in the last few hours. When we got news that one of Venom's upper management went missing, I just knew you were involved somewhere. What did you did do with Monroe?"

"Hooked him up to New York's power grid," I said, laughing bitterly at the morbid joke.

"Then I heard about what you did at the office building. How the hell could you do something like that, Charlotte? Do you even understand the ramifications of your actions? Christ almighty!" he thundered furiously.

"I'm sorry . . . I couldn't help myself. I became blood drunk . . . Couldn't stop even if I wanted to." I could feel the weight of the world pressing down on my young shoulders, smothering me with each passing moment.

"And now the entire fucking city is coming after you; the NYPD, Venom, even the damn Feds want your blood now." He angrily flicked the spent cigarette away and sighed deeply.

"So what do we do now?" I asked, running my fingers over the smooth edges of the silver mask in my hands. Why couldn't I just let it go? Throw it out of the shattered window and be done with it? *Because it's who you are.* The grim thought ran through my head. *It's all you will ever be.*

"First, you will have to lie low and wait for the heat to die down. Then we're going to get you out of New York City and out of the country. You cannot stay here. Not after the damage you've caused."

"I don't understand. Where are you taking me?" New York was the only place I had ever known, and I had never even been outside the city limits before the events leading up to the farmhouse. The fear of the unknown sent cold shivers down my spine as I watched one of the guards approach Vince and whisper something in his ear.

"It's best you don't know where yet. I had a talk with Richard and Peter, and they have a contact overseas who will give you refuge till I can sort out this ungodly mess you've caused. We're going to ship you out in a few weeks; we just need to make sure our contacts at the shipyards are taken care of and on board. You know you are complicating my life immensely, eh *bambina?*"

"Sorry . . ." I mumbled, too tired to pick a fight.

I just wanted to lay my head down somewhere, close my eyes, and hope it was all a bad dream when I woke up. *Fat chance of that happening.*

"And that is not the only problem I have to sort out. Oh, not even close," he said, closing his eyes and leaning his head on a nearby metal pole.

"What do you mean?"

"We will try to negotiate a peace treaty with Venom. I have no idea how the boss wants to manage that, but we will have to try. Maybe pay some sort of restitution for you taking out one of theirs. That's if they don't blow your brains out on sight, just on principle."

"They need me. I'm the only one with access to their entire database. I carry the genetic code in my body. They would not dare touch me." *False bravado, Charlotte? Really?*

"You would be surprised. You've become a damn liability to them, and I would not be surprised if they decide to cut their losses and just whack you on sight. That's what I would do."

"Wouldn't blame you if you did. Where are we going anyway?" I looked out of the broken window to see where I was, but to no avail. It must have been a rarely used line we took.

"I'm taking you to a safe house where they won't find you." His words were barely cold when I felt the subway train starting to lurch and slow down.

There was no station in sight, just the darkened walls of the subway line surrounding us.

"Quickly now, *bambina*. It won't take those sons of bitches upstairs long to figure out which direction we went. *Rapidamente!*" Vince and the two guards quickly exited the car, abandoning it in the middle of nowhere. The gravel crunched under our feet as we ran down the silent tunnel, fearful of hearing shouting and gunfire opening behind us.

"Where are we going?" I asked, my breathing steady, adrenaline under complete control, the only sounds the heartbeats around me. Perfect harmony in the midst of utter chaos.

"Almost there . . . Just a little bit further." Vince's eyes darted from side to side, looking for something. But what could it be?

"There it is!" he exclaimed and ran over to a side service entrance. Pausing for a moment, he placed his massive hands on the wheel of the hatch door and turned it. With a protesting groan of rusted steel, the wheel started spinning, and he opened the door.

"It pays to have people on the payroll." He suddenly tensed up as we heard shouting and the barking of dogs echoing down the tunnel. I could sense them, every thought, their hearts thumping against their chests. A bunch of beat cops scared out of their minds, they had no idea what they were dealing with. *Have to get away . . . get away before . . . No, Charlotte, don't think like that.*

"Everyone behind the door and keep your damned mouths shut." Vince bundled us through and slammed the door shut. Then came the longest wait of my life, hearing the approaching onrush of officers and dogs swarming outside. The big Mafioso threw his entire weight against the subway door and held on for dear life. Pearls of sweat ran down his forehead as we saw the door open, inch by agonizing inch.

Realizing he couldn't last, I placed my shoulder against the rusty door and tensed my body up. He looked over at me with rapidly widening eyes as the door remained steady, not moving another inch. It was barely a few seconds, but it felt like a lifetime that we held on.

Eventually, it fell quiet and the voices moved further down the tunnel. Finally, Vince relaxed and got up off the ground, dusting himself off. He looked at me silently, a look somewhere between trepidation and mistrust. I had never seen it from him before today, and it unsettled me somewhat.

"Right, follow me, but it keep down, understand?" he murmured, suddenly quieted down. We followed him down the service tunnel, ever deeper into the catacombs running beneath the streets of New York City. Past hissing pipes, trains thundering overhead, and cars hooting in the distance, he led us. How he knew the correct path to take was beyond me, but somehow he just knew. It must have been a good twenty to thirty-minute walk in the subterranean maze, but eventually he stopped and opened another steel door.

"We're here," he said, showing me inside.

"What is this place? I asked, looking around at the tiny room before my eyes.

"A safe house. Only the Mafia elite know about this." He hesitated for second, hoping that I had missed it. "You will stay here till we can move you. There is food in the fridge, a TV, and a radio to keep you company. The boys will keep guard at the door, making sure you are safe."

"So I'm a prisoner, is that it?" I said, turning around and looking him squarely in the eyes.

"Call it what you want, Charlotte. All I know is if you try to leave here, the boys are instructed to put a slug through your brain, no questions asked. *Capisce?*"

"Fuck you." My words, cold as ice, cut straight through him. He simply smiled, turned around, and walked away, slamming the steel door behind him. I was left alone again in my iron prison, my only company a scraggly looking black rat perched on a water pipe above me. Ignoring the creature, I switched on the TV and aimlessly switched between the channels.

Then I saw it.

A composite sketch of my face plastered all over CNN. The images of NYPD cruisers and FBI cars tearing up New York City flashed before my eyes.

Panic on the streets, people running around blindly, aimlessly as helicopters roamed overhead. A stoic-looking reporter droning soullessly on as they carried the bodies draped in white sheets from the office building. One after another, a gory procession of the dead. Never to be united with their families again.

They were already calling it the biggest manhunt in New York history, and there was talk of bringing in the National Guard. They already had a name for me.

The Huntress of Brooklyn. Cute nickname, I thought as another talking head flapped his gums on the screen. With a cool and precise kick, I smashed my foot through the TV screen and watched coldly as the orange sparks danced away into the dark corners of the room and the screen fell silent. Slowly, I walked over to the bed and lay down on it, staring up at the dripping pipes above my head. For the first time in what felt like ages, it became quiet around me again. The only sounds were the illicit scratching of the rat, the dripping of water, and the muffled voices of the two orangutans outside the door. I could think again, put things into clear perspective and just work things out. But inside, I knew that I could not stay any longer in New York City; it wasn't safe anymore. I had burnt that bridge the moment I left Monroe to die in a pile of his own filth. *You had no choice but to do it. Suck it up, princess.*

I kept wondering where they wanted to take me. Overseas, he

said, but where? *It's a pretty damn big place, and it could be frickin' Outer Mongolia for all you know, Charlotte.* I wasn't looking forward to the prospect of going off into the unknown and leaving my home behind. *Think of it as an adventure, and you might even get a tan out of it.* Mentally, I swore at the voice inside my head, telling it to shut up. With a huff, it disappeared, and I could finally settle down and get some rest. I just hoped the nightmares would leave me alone tonight. Just for one night.

That was all I asked.

To sleep, perchance to scream.

CHAPTER THIRTY

Severnaya Zemlya, Russia.

A cold watery sun had just risen over the vast expanses of the Siberian wilderness, casting dim rays over the frost-covered pine trees. The world was calm and at peace, like Mother Nature herself was resting gently, casting a distant eye on this forgotten part of creation. This was where I belonged, a girl apart in the majestic tundra of old Mother Russia. This was all I ever really knew, my soul in perfect harmony with the savageness of the forest, its icy heart beating as one with mine. I could never want for anything more in this life. This was my Garden of Eden, my paradise. For the past fifteen years, I have called this place home, ten of them spent alone. My father had passed on when I was fifteen years old; pneumonia claimed him one bitter -cold winter. But there was little time for mourning after I buried him; life in Siberia simply didn't allow sympathy or feeling sorry for yourself.

You had to carry on, no matter the circumstances, or perish in the process. *"Carry on and don't you dare look back. There is nothing for us back there."* Papa often told me that as he taught me how to survive and live off the land in the wilderness, to make it an ally in the darkest of times. I remembered with grim humor when I was sixteen and the social services people came to fetch me and drag me off to some foster family in Moscow. A few well-placed bear traps under the snow and a couple shots from my Simonov SKS carbine rifle soon sent them running for cover. They left me alone after that, figuring I was not worth the trouble or the risk of losing a limb. Truth be told, I hated using the rifle Papa left behind for me; there was no honor or satisfaction in using it. I preferred to stalk my prey in the ways of the old country, with bow and with knife. It was my way of showing respect to any animal I brought down. A way to connect with nature again.

But just because I didn't like using the rifle didn't mean I wasn't any good with it. I could go toe to toe with any Spetsnaz or sniper in the Russian military, be their equal on my worst day. But I chose not to fight, choosing instead the freedom of the forest. She gave me shelter and provided for my needs, gave me purpose in this world. In turn, I became her guardian, ridding the forest of any vermin that dared trespass there. This was my world, and I was content and happy. I could hear the soft dripping of late winter snow, the rustling of pine trees and the early morning calling of songbirds drifting on the icy wind. It was my favorite time to hunt—early morning when the air was clear and the world crisp around me. Stopping and sniffing the air, I caught a familiar scent. A pack of grey wolves had been moving through the southern reaches of the forest, and I had been tracking them for days now. The alpha had gone feral and had dragged a child away from a nearby village. I had to put the man-eater down before hunters from the surrounding areas came looking for him. *Don't need a bunch of trigger-happy idiots in my forest, and besides, I could do with a new winter coat,* I thought to myself, running my finger over the faint outlines of a wolf paw in the snow. The pack had been cautious, steering clear of any human settlement, too afraid of retribution after their nighttime attack on the village. I almost felt sorry for the alpha; he was just following his natural instincts, but I knew for the greater good that he had to go. There was no other option but to destroy him.

Going to have to hurry, there's a storm building to the east. Though the day was beautifully clear, I could sense the approach of the snowstorm. *Got to take down the alpha and find shelter before it hits.* Laughing softly to myself, I knew this was life in Siberia. Mother Nature always did the unexpected and always kept you on your toes. Kept you humble.

Pushing through the bough of a birch tree, I was about to start tracking the pack again when I stopped cold. Something was different and out of place this cold winter's morning. Something had strayed into my forest. Tying my blonde, almost snowlike hair tighter into a ponytail, I stretched my twenty-five-year-old frame out over the ground and closed my eyes. I could feel the vibrations of heavy machinery travelling along the floor of the forest.

"*Ty che blyad?*" It was those bitches from the local lumber company. It couldn't be anyone else. I thought I had made it clear to them last time around that this part of the forest was off-limits and there would be consequences for anyone caught trespassing in it. *Guess they didn't learn their lesson*, I thought to myself, thinking back to the carnage of broken logging machines I left behind after our last encounter. Silently swearing to myself, I looked back at the wolf trail leading off into the dark recesses of the forest. They would have to wait till after I'd dealt with the *mu'dak* hacking down my forest only a few hundred meters away.

Get going. As silent as the frost's whisper, I scythed wraithlike through the forest, closing in on my unsuspecting prey. *Glupyye lyudi. A blind man would be able to track them with all the noise they are making.* In a matter of minutes, I spotted their operation, ducking behind a large snow drift. The loggers had already hacked open a large swath of the forest, the cruel machines sawing and pulling mercilessly at my home while armed guards stood around carrying Kalashnikovs in their hands. It didn't matter to me if they were illegal or not; they had crossed the line of trees marked with a black cross. The locals had warned them: "Stay out of the southern reaches. There is a demon lurking there. You are looking for your death in her forest." But they didn't listen; their greed had made them blind and deaf to reasoning. And now they were going to pay for it.

Hunkered down behind the pile of snow, I felt the first flakes landing softly on my skin, their icy touch cool and calming. *Otlicho.* I folded my jacket inside out, the white material blending in perfectly with the surroundings, before reaching into my bag and folding a white piece of material around my face and hair.

Deep blue eyes peering from the material, I was ready for action. Just had to wait a few minutes. The goddess of the forest soon obliged as the snow started falling heavier, blocking visibility in a sheet of pure white.

Unsheathing my Kizlyar hunting knife, I ghosted through the tree line, moving like a terrible thought, cold and uncaring. My only goal their destruction.

From the ashen gloom, I appeared before the first guard; disarming him before he could breathe. His eyes stretched wide in horror. I severed the deltoid muscles of both arms, hearing him scream in agony as he flopped helplessly on the ground. A second guard came running, trying desperately to see through the bellowing rage of the storm. The knife left my hand perfectly, striking him center mass, puncturing a lung, streams of bright red blood gushing out over the crisp white snow as I pulled my knife from the hapless guard.

"Keep pressure on the wound and you will live," I said in his ear, feeling his terrified body shaking on the ground. Despite my rage, I wasn't here to kill anyone. *Just want them gone from my forest.* Breaking and flinging the AK47 into the bushes, I saw one of the loggers trying to escape. Screaming like a stuck pig, his voice was clear even through the storm. Calmly I reached for the bow on my back and nocked an arrow.

Taking a deep breath in the midst of the chaos surrounding me, I let loose two arrows in quick succession. The flight was true as it whistled through the air, lodging deep into both his kneecaps, pinning him to a nearby tree. Another one came at me from behind, swinging a logging axe wildly in the air. There was no rage, no anger in my movements, just the calm feeling of being in perfect sync with nature as I easily dodged his attacks, moving like a whisper around him. The *ublyudok* never had a chance as I disarmed him with consummate ease before delivering a thundering blow to his throat with the axe handle. Gasping for air and clutching his throat, I knelt down beside him, comforting the fallen logger as he squirmed in pain.

"Relax and breathe. I haven't fractured your throat." Leaving his writhing body behind in the snow, I walked over to the metal siding hut. There was one person left—the foreman of the operation. Kicking open the steel door with cruel efficiency, I saw the thin, bearded man hunched over in the corner, pointing a Makarov directly at my head. We stared at each other for what felt like hours as I watched the pistol in his hand shaking and trembling. Slowly, I walked forward and took the weapon from him, folding my hand around the grey steel butt of the pistol. I knew he didn't have the guts to fire on me.

"Enough." My words were cold and uncompromising as I took him by the collar and dragged him into the middle clearing of the camp. The storm subsided, and he looked around in horror at the brutal sight of his men broken and scattered around him. I unwrapped the cloth around my head and let my long blond hair fall free.

"A girl . . . You are a girl . . . *Bozhe moi!*" he stammered with a heavy Russian accent, scarcely believing the figure standing mere inches away from him.

"I want you to remember that. Today, a girl showed you mercy. Now take your men, get in your Jeeps, and leave this place. All your equipment belongs to me now, and if you dare come back here, I will visit a hell upon you that you dare not believe."

Staggering backwards, the foreman sprawled in the snow before picking himself up and rushing over to his fallen men. I watched coldly as he dragged the wounded to the Jeeps and piled them in. With a puff of black dust, they roared down the frozen dirt path and were soon gone from sight. I was left alone again, and a silence had fallen on the clearing once more. Taking my time, I severed the fuel lines of each mechanical monster and threw a lit match in afterwards. Then, just as quietly as I appeared, I left the logging camp, a thick black trail of smoking machines the only evidence that I had been there. Others would come in time, but for now, the forest was safe again.

The snowstorm had wiped out the tracks of the wolf pack, and it was getting on in the day. I would return in the morning to pick up the trail again; they would not move far in the night. Just before sunset, I made it back home. A modest wooden hut deep in the forest with a rack of wolf and bear skins on the front porch, it was home to me. As I approached through the tree line, the now familiar feeling of something out of place took hold of me again. There was a set of snowmobile tracks in the snow, and someone had lit a fire in the chimney inside.

Kakogo cherta? Reaching for an axe used for firewood, I slowly approached the wooden hut, checking every inch around me for an ambush. But everything remained eerily calm. Reaching the rough wooden door, I carefully inched it open. There was a man, barely in his forties with slicked back hair and a very fashionable hunting outfit sitting inside with a cup of coffee in his hand. His skin was tanned and well taken care of, smooth with the slightest nick under the right eye.

"Who the hell are you?" I asked, gripping the axe tightly in my hands.

He simply smiled, flashing a set of perfect teeth, and pushed a brown manila envelope to me before speaking in perfect Russian: "Lyudmila Pavlichenko, the time has come. We are in need of your services now. You need to bring your sister home."

CHAPTER THIRTY-ONE

New York City.

Two weeks in this hellhole. This prison had become my home, my only point of reference of who I am, who I was. Barely clinging onto the last vestiges of sanity, I spent my days training, staring at the walls, fighting the demons in my mind. There would be days where I would drive them back into the shadows, watching them run in panic before my eyes. And then there would be days where they would get the better of me.

I would spend hours, days maybe, howling at the damp subway walls, my lonely voice echoing down the empty corridors. I sometimes wondered if anyone apart from the two assholes outside my door could hear me, maybe the bums living in the tunnels or the maintenance crews working underground. Could they understand my frenetic ramblings as I scratched and clawed at the brick walls, streams of blood running down my torn fingers? Did they whisper to themselves that there was a tortured demon living in the darkest corners of the subway? I would not know. It was just me and my prison cell.

About five days ago—who can really tell time down here anyway—was the worst. All the bloody and maimed faces of all the souls I had slaughtered came back to me in one night. I could hear the shouting, the blood gurgling in their throats as they begged mercy from me. I threw myself against the walls, harder which each ragged scream, scarlet streaming down my mouth while I pummeled my fists hopelessly against brick and steel, anything to just make the voices stop.

"Go away . . . go away." The words repeated as I lay on the cement floor, near vegetative, that blurry line between alive and dead. Which one was I? Maybe both? Maybe neither? I could not find the answer, watching the subway rats scurry away with a strand of drool hanging from my mouth. Insanity took over me as I began laughing louder, shrieks of madness a symphony of my own demented despair. Crawling over with broken fingernails to the shards of glass left over from the TV I smashed, I held the wicked edges in my trembling hands, seeing my broken reflection in them.

And then came the first suicide attempt.

I felt the glass shard cut into my flesh, a red line forming across my veins as I willed it to release me. Just to finally let all my pain and agony go. I didn't give a damn about heaven and hell anymore. My hell was the prison cell of my mind, and I yearned to be free, no matter the cost. I was so close now, just had to watch myself bleed out and it would all be over. But even then I was denied. Gazing with tears running down my cheeks, I saw the wound close before my eyes, torn flesh healing before my horrified eyes. The monster inside me would not let go. No, it was not done torturing me. It seemed like we still had a distance to journey together, no matter what.

Two days later, as I lay in a pile of my own blood, puke, and piss, a feeling of acceptance for what I had done came over me. There was no taking back what I had done, no redemption for my actions, but the simple feeling that I had no choice but to soldier on.

Slowly getting to my feet and stripping off the green, soaked clothing I had on, I sat naked and cross-legged on the moth-eaten bed, watching a rat nibble on some crumbs left behind in the corner. He seemed so at peace, despite his circumstances. We were both in the same shit, and we had no choice but to deal with whatever came before us. As he pawed frantically at the small pieces of cheese and stale bread on the floor, I closed my eyes and started searching for calmness inside. For the first time, I could hear another voice in my head. But this one was different, more soothing and calm in the way it spoke to me. The message was simple, but it started resonating with me somewhere deep inside my fractured mind, cutting through the darkness.

You can't fix this, Charlie, but you can stop the bleeding. Purge the poison and kill the evil. And then I knew what I had to do. The meeting. The head of Venom was going to be out in the open. *One last kill before I disappear and bury the monster inside me.* One final act of defiance, and nobody would ever hear of Charlotte Corday again. Closing my eyes, I could hear the iron key rattling in the lock and one of the guards, the small, ratlike one with too much cologne came in. He was carrying a metal serving tray in his hands, shuffling closer.

Escape, Charlie.

"Jesus Christ, would you look at this fucking mess," he mumbled to himself as he cautiously approached me, stepping carefully through pools of stagnant blood and puke.

Escape, Charlie.

"Hey, you alive in there, bitch? Why you all naked?" The rat poked me with a stubby finger, unsure of what to make of the serene figure sitting in front of him.

Escape, Charlie!

"I said—" He never got a chance to finish his sentence as I grabbed his wrist, breaking it , his screams of pain instantly muted, the metal serving tray slamming into his face, knocking him out cold. As he fell, I pulled his sidearm from his belt, sending two shots flying at the door. I knew the second guard, the gorilla, would come charging in as soon as he heard the commotion inside. The bullets struck true; double tap to the chest, dropping the guard. It was over before the rat could scurry away. He sat quietly in the corner, crumbs of cheese on his whiskers as he calmly watched me step over the still twitching body of the first guard and kneel at the second one. Tearing off a strip of material from his overcoat, I held it firmly down on the wound.

"Where is the meeting?" I hissed through gritted teeth, cradling his head under my hand.

"Fuck you." He spat the words out, blood running down his chin.

"Listen very carefully, I won't repeat it. You have two options: one, you can tell me where and when the meeting between your boss and Venom takes place, and you will live to see the spawn you call a family grow up one day. Or you take option two: I take the pressure off the wound and you take the chance your little friend wakes up in time before you bleed out. I don't know about you, but the rats down here look damn hungry to me. Being alive while the vermin eat you limb from limb . . . it's a shitty way to go. What will it be?"

The Mafioso thought long and hard about it, looking me deep in the eyes. No matter how tough you think you are, the specter of death, the thought of meeting the pale rider would bring any man to his knees. Finally he nodded, wheezing and rasping the words at me with great strain and effort. "The boss never told us where the meeting was going to take place; all we know is that it is two days from now. You have to believe me!"

"I do." I smiled and tapped him on the cheek. "But if I ever find any of you in my city again, my face will be the last thing you ever see. Now, go live your life and harm no man." I stood up from the fallen thug and headed back to the first one.

Still breathing. Good, I thought before stripping the clothing from him. My luck was in; he was exactly my size. Looking over my shoulder at the carnage as I exited the room, I saw the rat still sitting in the corner. With a wry smile, I winked at it before heading into the darkness of the subway system.

Got to think clearly, can't make a mistake now. My heart beat steady as I threaded my way through the maze system of tunnels running under the city. *Can't go home; they will be watching that for sure. The theatre is out as well. Got to stay away from public places for as long as I can. Where, Charlotte. Where?* I kept thinking to myself, fighting to figure it out. *The old boxing gym, nobody knows about it. It's my only chance. Just hope nobody has moved in or found my stash.* I kept a Dragunov sniper rifle there, borrowed from my uncles. Never thought I would use it; it was just for emergencies.

Pretty big damn emergency here, Charlotte, the voice in my head said as I ducked down a side tunnel.

Shut up you. I couldn't afford to drop my concentration even for a moment. There was no telling if there were still any NYPD officers down here looking for me. Unlikely, but no sense in taking an unneeded risk. It seemed quiet, the only sounds the dripping of pipes and the grating of iron wheels in the distance. I ran into a couple of bums living down here in the darkness. For a moment I thought they would recognize me, but they simply went on with their business. Maybe they'd heard my screams echoing through the tunnels; maybe they thought I was just another lost soul like them. I soon left them behind, the denizens of the night. It felt surreal seeing other people down here, the truly forgotten ones.

Using my senses, I quickly made my way through the miles of tunnels and service routes, carefully waiting for subway trains to thunder past before carrying on. For a moment, I swear a driver saw me as he flashed past.

It doesn't matter. You will be long gone before he can report it in. Stay focused.

Hours later by my reckoning, I came to a service ladder leading up to the street above. Night had already fallen, but the city was sleeping uneasily, waiting for the demon to show up again.

Might as well. Carefully, I scaled up the ladder and pushed the heavy manhole cover to the side. Not daring to breathe, I raised my head up and looked around. My luck was still holding for the time being.

Not bad, Charlotte. Not bad at all. I was less than a mile away from the gym; got to make a run for it.

Folding my collar up, I emerged back into the city. It felt weird to be back, but I couldn't afford any of that now. Reaching the gym was the only priority. Moving like a ghost between the buildings, I kept looking around, expecting to see cops and Feds around every corner, but everything stayed deadly quiet. The boxing gym loomed at the end of the block, faded signs of glory years long past lit up in shades of yellow from the streetlights.

Still boarded up. Good. In seconds, I reached the gym and pulled the boards back, cringing at every Judas-like creak of the graffiti-encrusted boards. The place was inky black, the smell of dust and decay hanging heavy in the air, but it seemed empty.

Fumbling for the light switch, the gym was soon bathed in dim, white light.

I should have felt his presence there. How could I have missed it? *Stupid, stupid.* I swung around as I heard his voice, my pistol already out and aimed at his head. I saw the smirking figure sitting on the apron of the ring, cleaning his nails with a penknife.

"Hello, Charlie. It's been a while."

It's not possible. It's just not possible.

Like a bad dream, he had come back into my life.

The ghost of my demented past had returned.

Victor was alive.

CHAPTER THIRTY-TWO

"What the hell are you doing here? How did you find this place?" I kept my pistol trained on his head, the aim steady and true.

"You're not exactly subtle are you, Charlotte? You really need to learn how to lose a tail," he replied sardonically, flicking closed the penknife in his hand and jumping lightly off the apron.

"I said, what do you want, Victor?" Dirty and sore from my ordeal in the subway, I was in no mood to play games.

"Just wanted to see what happened to little miss badass. You look tired, kid. Have you been getting enough sleep?"

"Screw you. You have exactly five seconds to get out of here before I tattoo your brains on the wall. One . . ." I started counting, finger itching on the pistol's trigger.

"Still such a hot head. You haven't changed much since we ran into each other at Yankee Stadium. Nice move with the pitching machine by the way. I didn't see that one coming."

"Two . . ."

"And then what, Charlie? You going to kill me as well? Just another notch on your bloodstained wall, is that it?" He reached for a cigarette and lit it, taking his time as the grey smoke drifted upwards toward the gym's roof.

"One more kill and I'm out." Victor just stood there, seemingly unperturbed by my presence or the gun pointed at him. *What is he doing here? Why hasn't he tried to kill me yet?*

"Then little Charlotte is going to ride off into the sunset and never be seen again. Maybe even start a family far away from here." The sarcasm was thick in his voice as he puffed deeply on the cheap cigarette.

"Wasn't planning that far ahead," I replied, eyeing him suspiciously.

"You are fooling yourself, little one. We cannot change who we are. You and I are just instruments in this pathetic power game they play. Do you think anything will be different once you put a bullet through the head of Venom's CEO?"

"How did you—"

"Please. It was not difficult to figure out their plans. Not after your less-than-restrained rampage. You pushed them into a corner, Venom and the Mafia, and this was the only recourse they had left. Either make peace or watch New York City burn further." Victor reached over to a case next to him and pulled out the Dragunov. With a snarl, I let fly a round in his direction. It whizzed by his head, but he didn't move an inch. Just tapping the cigarette ash to the ground and looking over the sniper rifle.

"So what? I don't give a damn about their politics or peace deals." A drop of sweat dripped down my finger as Victor simply smiled and tossed the rifle at me.

"You are the counterpoint, the very center of their worlds. The one that started all this shit, and the one that can end it. But you got to ask yourself, can you live with yourself once you pull that trigger?"

"What do you mean?" I asked, putting the sniper rifle on the floor, never taking my eyes off him for a second.

"Once you see brains scattered on the pavement, be it Venom or Mafia, can you live with yourself? You're going to become exactly like me, just a shell, a broken toy discarded by whoever thought you were special once. These bastards are going to use you till there is nothing left of you inside anymore." No matter how hard he tried to hide it behind false bravado, I could see the intense pain and suffering in Victor's eye.

"So what do you suggest I do? Walk away and pretend like all of this never happened? Is that it?" My voice raised, I could barely contain my rage, wanting so badly to put a slug through his damned head.

"You got to make a choice, Charlotte," he replied, testing and probing my reactions.

"A choice?"

"In a few days, you will have both of them in your sights. The CEO of Venom or the head of the Italian Mafia in New York. The ones that ruined your life and stole your childhood or the ones that are playing you for all you are worth. Choices, choices, which one will it be?"

"And if I don't want to make that choice? Who's to say I won't just pack up everything and run as far as my legs will carry me?"

Victor lowered his head, shielding his eye from me before replying. "Because we were born to be killers, and nothing we can do can change that. That and you will always have the regret that you had the opportunity to stop pure evil but never took it. The regret will kill you in the end, much quicker than any of their bullets will."

For the first time, I lowered my pistol and sighed deeply before putting it away. What made me do it, I will never know. Perhaps I recognized a kindred spirit in Victor, someone just as damaged and broken as I was. Gently, I placed my hand on his shoulder, feeling his body tensing up as he tried to move away.

"Why did you come here?" I asked with compassion in my voice, instantly feeling sorry for the hunched-up figure before me, all illusions of brashness and arrogance now gone from him. He looked up at me, fighting back the tears rolling down his cheeks.

"Because I cannot see you become me. Can't you understand that? I was never strong enough to stand up to them, but you . . . you are different. There is the spirit of a warrior inside you, not that shit Venom pumped into you, but real heart. You are the only one of us that can break free from their grasp and live your life like it's supposed to be. Whatever choice you make in a few days, I've got to know that there is still something human left inside you, that they didn't take everything you have. I have to know this . . ."

I sat down on the edge of the boxing ring and held Victor's black hair in my hands, his face downward in grief. Looking off into the murky corners of the gym, seeing faded fight posters on the walls, I bit my lip hard, holding back the emotions inside me.

"After all I've done . . ." I whispered slowly. "After all the blood I've shed, how can you call me human?"

"Because you are my sister and I love you." His hands held mine tightly, too afraid to let go even for a second. I could feel his body shake as I held him . Maybe it was mere minutes, but it felt like an eternity that we united again. All our anger and sorrows melted away till there was nothing left but two vulnerable souls caught up in something so much bigger than either of us could understand.

I looked Victor deep in his eye and thought hard for a moment before speaking. "I'm leaving New York City once all this is over with. Why don't you come with me? The arrangements have already been made for my escape, but I'm sure there is space for you as well."

Victor smiled sadly, putting his hand on the side of my face before stepping back. "I can't. This will always be the place where I belong. Born in this hellhole, and they will find me dead here one day in some godless alley somewhere, going out like a king overdosing on smack or some shit like that. And besides, somebody has to stay behind and keep these bitches busy while you make a run for it."

"Don't say that . . ." I felt my brother's hands slip from mine, watched him fade from me.

"I've lived longer than I should have, and I've made the most of the time given to me. I can die happily knowing I finally found my sister and that she is going to be just fine. I just wish I could be there to see you grow up, for the person you are and the person you can be one day. You are going to be truly amazing."

"No, Victor, no . . . I can't lose you, not again, not like this." The walls I had built so carefully around me for years, never allowing anyone to come even near them, came tumbling down.

For the first time in my life, no matter how brief it was, I realized that I was not alone. That there was someone just like me out there.

Victor bent down and placed the sniper rifle in my hands before kissing me on the forehead. "Give 'em hell, kid, but never forget who you are. Love you, sis." Slowly, he turned and walked away, black coat flapping in the gloom as he looked back one last time. I watched the city swallow him whole again. I would never see my brother again, but it gave me a renewed sense of hope that he was out there fighting for me.

You have to carry on, Charlie. It's what he would have wanted for you. I knew the voice in my head was right. In a few precious days, I would have to take responsibility for my actions, and I would be the one to pull the trigger. Which one of the evils, Venom or Mafia, would fall I didn't know yet, but time would tell. No matter what choice I made, my life would change completely. *You just have to own it, Charlie. All on you now.* I walked back into the gym and packed the Dragunov away in its case, not wanting to see it till the day of reckoning finally arrived. It was a somber evening, all by myself as I lay alone in the center of the boxing ring, staring up at the ceiling and thinking deeper thoughts than any teenager ever should have. Victor, my godparents, Vince—they all crossed my mind through the evening. I wondered how my choices would affect their lives, for the better or the worse.

For their sakes, you have to do this. And then for the first time, I managed to smile. The thought that someone out there believed in me, in who I was—not the feared assassin but simply Charlie, the girl from New York—gave me hope that everything was going to be all right. That no matter the darkness waiting for me out there, I could handle it.

I finally fell asleep in the middle of the boxing ring, legs curled up and my eyes closed in peace finally achieved. The city held its breath around me, awaiting with a quiet hush for the next chapter of this strange tale to unfold.

The story of the girl with rifle in hand versus a great evil. Of the supreme choice she had to make in a few breathless days.

But come what may, I was ready.

CHAPTER THIRTY-THREE

Have to get out of here. It felt like the walls of the boxing gym were closing in on me, and I needed some fresh air, danger be damned. I took the chance and ventured out into the city again, head tucked away under a cloth hood. The streets were tense, everyone holding their breath, looking over their shoulders for any signs of the huntress. I couldn't blame them; it had been a horrific act on my part, and one for which there could never be any redemption. All I could do was to pull the trigger one more time, then disappear for good. One choice to make before it was all over.

I thought about the choice as my face was bathed in blue and red police lights flashing past. Why couldn't it just have been simple? Pick one fucker and send him straight to hell, easy as that. Why was I so conflicted? Venom screwed up my entire life; they were responsible for all this, for the monster lurking inside me. The head of the damned organization out in the open, I knew this was a rare opportunity which I couldn't afford to waste.

You got him in your sights. Do it, Charlotte. The voice urged me on, resolutely speaking to my very inner core. One shot, one scarlet splash of brains on cold cement and it was all over. The rest of Venom would crumble and scatter without his leadership. *So very easy.* But then I thought of the other side of the coin, the second part of the complex equation—a chance to silence the Italian Mafia, deal them a crippling blow before disappearing under their noses.

They used you, Charlotte, just like everybody else. Think of all the pain and suffering they caused to thousands of people, including you. I headed past steaming Chinese restaurants, kitchen staff sitting idly on the steps smoking, the places eerily quiet for a late afternoon in New York City. There was talk on the radio of the mayor declaring a curfew in the city but nothing had yet been declared. *You can drop that fat bastard with one simple act; imagine how good it would feel to see him writhing in a pool of his own blood on the ground.* I'll admit that the thought did strike a chord with me, that it would be the perfect chance to cut the head off the snake. Stopping for a moment as a hot dog vendor eyed me suspiciously before wheeling his cart farther down the street, something else occurred to me.

Why not kill them both? Set the whole nest of vipers on fire and watch them burn. The voice in my head seemed in a particularly vicious mood, but I dismissed it immediately. If I played my cards correctly, I could make it seem like one side turned on the other. They would destroy each other while I slipped away in the chaos. Easy as that.

Nice one, Charlotte. Let the rats sort it out between themselves.

Shut up, voice. I needed to clear my head and there was something else bothering me. Vince. Every time something happened to me, he was somehow always around. How was that possible? I had kept pushing it to the back of my mind these past few weeks, not wanting to think about it. But now I had no choice in the matter; I had to get some answers before I took the shot. The question was how to find him in a city of millions of people?

Listen for his heartbeat; he's out there somewhere. The voice chimed in and was gone before I could say anything. I felt it was right; I had to find Vince and quickly. Time was running out. Ducking down a side alley, I scaled up a fire escape as the sun started to wane and set behind the skyscrapers of old New York. People started taking down laundry and closing windows, afraid of the bogeyman roaming the night. I stood alone on the roof, the sun shining orange on my tired face as I closed my eyes and started to listen. So many voices, millions chattering into the void. Their heartbeats . . . scared . . . rapidly beating as they rushed home to beat the night. *Concentrate . . . Listen for his dark heart . . . Concentrate.* Through the turmoil of my mind and the city I sifted, discarding pulse after pulse till finally I found him. Only a few blocks away, his heartbeat elevated, shards of adrenaline in his blood.

What are you up to? I thought to myself, standing on the ledge and staring off into the rapidly fading distance. Taking a deep breath, I took a few steps backwards and ran toward the edge, launching myself across the chasm. The huntress was on the move, stalking her prey.

Is he really your prey, Charlotte? Or just somebody caught up in the madness of your life? I had to find out as I willed my legs to move faster. Building to building I ran, ducking and diving, ever closer to my target.

Around me, silence; no rushing of cars or trains, of people talking, hearts beating. Just the rapid pumping of Vince's heart. I came to a stop, looking down and seeing him walking far below. He wasn't alone but was surrounded by three others an equal distance apart, moving as one with him.

Bodyguards.

Now what is a low-level mob enforcer doing with three guards around him? I wondered as I saw him head into a nearby building for a few brief minutes. He didn't waste time before returning and climbing back inside a waiting Town Car. It moved slowly, carefully down the street. I gave chase, keeping the car in constant eyesight. The rooftops were my highway across the city, the perfect road for those that do not wish to be spotted. I followed them for hours across the city; deep into the night we went. Were they following a pattern or was it simple paranoia? A fear of the viper mere days away from the peace meeting perhaps? Either way, they were slowly working their way towards Midtown. Half an hour later, they reached their destination.

The Manhattan Plaza. It had to be the location of the meeting. The roof was the perfect spot, open space with plenty of exits around. I watched with deepening interest as the Continental pulled up and Vince got out. He spoke briefly with his three guards before they moved out in different directions, leaving him behind.

What are you up to . . . Oh, that is clever. It was a scouting trip. Vince was setting up the meeting spot in his favor, placing snipers at all angles overlooking the plaza. Taking my time, I took notice of their exact positions on the nearby rooftops, especially the one on the top floor of the Plaza Hotel. His heart was beating like a jackhammer and I could pinpoint his exact location with ease. Vince wasn't taking any chances in his dealings with Venom. Twenty-odd minutes later, they were finished and back at the car. I had seen enough for the night as I watched the Lincoln exit the Plaza parking garage and speed off into the distance. Looking up at the nearby Plaza Hotel, another thought came to me.

If I can take out the sniper there, it should give me a clean view of the meeting. I could even use the sniper's own rifle against the head of Venom. The type of round that should be easy to trace and that could set off a war between them. Perfect.

So that's it then? You've made up your mind, Charlotte, that Venom has to die? The voice seemed distant and, for the first time, almost unsure of itself as I walked over to the roof of the parking garage. A cold wind ruffled my hair as I judged the distances and sightlines, making sure every variable was taken care of. There was no space for errors, no second chances.

One shot, one kill. Running my hand over the unfeeling cement, I imagined who would be standing here in only a few days, seeing their expressions through my sniper scope. Would there be anger, pain, resentment, or hatred in their eyes? Shock when the first bullet hits home?

You're over thinking this again; get some rest now for God's sake, I admonished myself, pulling the hood angrily over my head again. But then again, who could sleep at a time like this? The adrenaline was pumping through my veins, steady and controlled. My senses heightened to the world around me, taking in every subtle nuance, every detail of my environment till I became almost as one with the location.

There was one more thing I had to do before the night was over, one more act before I could lay my head down in restless sleep. I had to connect with someone again, just to feel human again. To not feel so damn alone anymore. With one last look over my shoulder, I exited the parking garage, past the sleeping guard in his booth. I saw a couple of people leaving the Plaza Hotel and getting into waiting Yellow Cabs. Maybe they were tired of being afraid, or perhaps they simply didn't know or care about the monster lurking in the streets of New York City. It was weird, but somehow it stayed with me as I walked the streets deep in thought. I found a pay phone a few blocks down, closing the grimy glass door behind me and paging through the torn phone book inside, finally finding the number I was looking for.

Winter Garden Theatre 2122396200. The phone rang distantly as I looked around me, the paranoia still palpable in me, always alert, always waiting for the next danger lurking around the corner. A disinterested voice chimed, interrupting my thoughts.

"Winter Garden Theatre reception, how may I help you? For bookings and enquiries, please phone in the morning," the voice droned on melancholically.

"Yes, is Richard there? I need to talk to him," I replied, suddenly thinking that this was a stupid and ill thought-out idea. Just as I was about to hang up, the voice responded.

"He's backstage finishing up a production of *West Side Story.* I'll see if he is available. Who shall I say is calling?"

"It's his, uh . . . niece. I'll hold, thank you." I grimaced at the blunt-faced lie, closing my eyes and tapping the receiver softly on my forehead while I waited. A few minutes later, a familiar voice sounded, rich and full of life like I had known and loved.

"Who is this? Speak up quickly now; you are rudely interfering with my drinking time."

I hesitated for a moment before speaking. "It's me, Charlie. I'm sorry I called . . . I shouldn't have . . ." I wanted to hang up and walk away, but his voice brought me back, the handset suspended motionlessly in my quivering hand.

"Dahling, is that really you? My God, what is going on?" I could hear the concern in his voice, and it felt like my heart was being ripped apart.

"I . . . I need to talk to you. I'm in deep trouble, and I don't know what to do. I'll understand if you don't want anything to do with me; please don't tell Peter I called." I was waiting for him to slam the phone down, for another person to reject me, throw me away like a piece of trash along the highway. But he didn't; his voice still as clear and resolute as ever.

"I'll slip out while he is working on set design. The old fool gets so preoccupied with his work, I bet he wouldn't even notice if Hannibal himself was holding his nuts while doing it. Meet me at the Bow Bridge in Central Park, ten o'clock tomorrow morning, and we can talk. Are you okay, dahling? We're sick with worry over here."

"I'm fine, but we'll talk tomorrow. I have to go." I hung up and stood motionlessly in the phone booth, a small smile forming on my face. Someone out there still hadn't given up on me; someone still believed in me. After everything I had done,

Uncle Richard was still there for me. It was almost unbelievable.

I was not alone.

The streets suddenly seemed less cold, less distant as I slowly walked back to the gym, the night a blanket of lights wrapped around me. A million thoughts ran through my head, so much to think of, so much to make sure of before the big day finally arrived.

One shot, one kill. One choice to make.

Get some rest, Charlie; you're going to need it.

CHAPTER THIRTY-FOUR

What are you doing, Charlotte? I must have asked myself that question a million times the previous night. I barely got any sleep at all, tossing and turning on the makeshift bed in the boxing ring. *You shouldn't have involved Richard and Peter; you've been nothing but a burden on them.* Was this regret or guilt causing my insomnia?

Maybe both, who knows? I just wish things weren't always so damn complicated.

"You cannot go it alone; they're the only family you got," the voice chided me softly, but I knew it was right. Not that I deserved it, but they stuck with me; through everything I had done, my uncles were there for me. Gently resting my head on the ring post, I closed my eyes and made up my mind. I had to see my uncle, damn the risks.

I left the gym just after nine in the morning, taking my time as I made my way down to Central Park. Head tucked in a grey hoodie, I could feel the paranoia building up inside me; like there were a million eyes on me. They were all watching, waiting for my next move. I just wanted it to be over. Was that too much to ask?

"*One shot and you're gone. Nobody in this city will ever see you again. Just keep it together for a little bit longer.*" I still couldn't figure out if the voice was the reason for my insanity or simply taking me deeper into the maelstrom of my life. Shaking my head, I reached the park a short while after, cautiously entering deeper into the leafy green expanse. A few people were doing aerobics on the lawns, others throwing a Frisbee around. I stalked past a group of runners, never lifting my head, hoping nobody recognized me. There was no running, no escape if they raised the alarm. I would barely make it a few blocks before they took me down. Bullet to the skull, bleeding out on the pavement; nobody to care, nobody to give a damn as I faded away.

"*Keep your head down. Almost there.*" It was quiet near the bridge when I reached it; a cooing couple strolled past me, ice creams in hand, while a vendor set up his cart at the far end of the pond. I was early, exactly like I had planned it. Wanted to make sure there wasn't any unwelcome company around. It was a gorgeous summer morning in New York City, and as I was standing behind a nearby tree, I felt human, even if it was just for a few precious moments.

Maybe you can come back here one day when all this has blown over. Start a life again, perhaps. The words were hollow, and I knew I was fooling myself; after tomorrow, there would be no going back. Once I pulled that trigger, I would be marked for death; no matter which side I chose. There would always be someone waiting for me to return to New York City, waiting to end my life. A refugee from my own country, always on the run.

Never look back. Never again.

Just before ten, I saw him. Richard scurried up to the bridge, looking around the whole time. I waited a few minutes to see if anybody was watching him. No, he was alone. Biting my lip, I exited from behind the tree and walked over to him.

What am I going to say? What can I say? I stood behind him for a few seconds, watching his hunched-over figure as he leaned over the railing. It seemed like he had aged many a year in only a few weeks and like he was carrying the world on his shoulders.

"Richard," I said softly and watched him turn around as if in slow motion. There were tears in his eyes as he embraced me warmly.

"Hey, dahling . . . I missed you," he whispered through the tears, not wanting to let go even for an instant. Finally, he stepped back and fished a handkerchief from his pocket, dabbing at his eyes.

"Let me look at you. You look good, kid." He tried to smile, but I could see the sadness on his face. He couldn't hide it, no matter how hard he tried.

"I'm holding on best as I can. Can we go sit somewhere and talk?" I replied, putting my hand on his shoulder as we headed to a park bench a distance away from the crowds. I slumped forward, head in hands while we sat in silence for a few minutes. Finally, Richard spoke up, staring off into the distance.

"What's going on, kid? You know you can always talk to me, so help me to understand what is happening to you." He took my hand in his, holding tightly as I tried to pull away.

"I got in with the wrong crowd and I messed up. I don't know what to do." I could feel all the old demons coming back to me, their nightmarish features dancing before my mind's eye again.

"It was you that killed all those people in the office block, wasn't it?"

I nodded, too ashamed to look him in the eyes. "It was. How . . . how is Peter taking it?"

"Not good, dahling, not good at all. He's hurting badly, even though he is trying to not show it. We had a big fight about it the other day. He feels hurt and betrayed by what you did. I could see he wanted to push you away, have nothing to do with you. But I managed to talk him down for the time being."

"Thank you. I don't deserve your kindness. Not one little bit," I replied, feeling even more ashamed now than before.

"It's not about deserving anything, dahling. It's just that family has to stick together, no matter what. I won't lie to you, what you did . . . Jesus, kiddo . . . I spent many a night sitting and thinking of why I should forgive you. Oh man . . ."

"For what I've done, there can be no forgiveness." My heart was heavy as I spoke the words, but I knew it was true. I had crossed the line and gone too far. There was no redemption for me.

"I know, dear. There will always be a part of me that believes that. But your uncle and I, we decided we are going to stick with you, even if just for a little while longer," he said, a pained smile forming on his weathered face.

"What do you mean?" I asked, turning and looking at him.

"I talked to Cousin Mickey on the phone, and he is willing to take you in. We're going to smuggle you out of the country in a shipping container."

"A shipping container?" I couldn't believe what he was saying to me, thinking that he must have lost his mind.

"It's the best and only way to get you through customs. They will be watching the borders and airports carefully, especially after the shit you pulled. No, there is no other option for you, my dear. I already talked to a contact at the ports and they have taken care of everything. There will be a new passport waiting, if needed, and we even got you extra water and food for your journey. You're all set; we leave at four o'clock from the theatre to get you shipping out at five p.m." He paused for a moment, looking me deep in the eyes. "But there was something else, right? That's why you wanted to meet me here."

I nodded, standing up, trying to find the correct words. "I have to do one more thing before I leave, and I don't know how to say this." It was killing me inside, and I knew it was going to hurt Richard terribly.

"Just say it, dear. I'm a big girl; I can handle it." Why did he have to be so damn calm about it? Why couldn't he just shout and scream at me? That, at least, I knew how to handle. I tapped a tree trunk with an open palm a few times, not looking back before speaking up.

"I have to hurt one more person. I don't have a choice in the matter." God, I hated myself for saying those words. I felt my soul shatter with every syllable uttered.

"What? No, dahling, no . . ." I didn't have to look around; I could feel the pain and shock on his face. It took every bit of strength I had left in me to carry on.

"I have to. There is a chance to stop a great evil tomorrow, even just to slow it down a bit. I have to do this . . ."

"But why you? Who decided that it should be you to do this?" Richard's voice broke, raw emotion streaming through it.

I swung around, fighting back the tears. "Because I am the only one left who can pull the trigger. If I walk away, a lot more people are going to get hurt, and I cannot allow that."

"Is this how you get redemption, Charlotte?" It was the first time Richard had called me by my name. It hit me like a hammer blow.

"There is no redemption for me. Just maybe a chance to do the right thing for once in my life," I replied, turning to walk away. He reached and took my hand in his, sighing deeply as I shielded my eyes from him.

"We'll carry you home, dahling, no matter the cost. Just promise me one thing; can you do that for me?"

"What? Name it," I replied, lifting my eyes to his.

"When you reach your destination, promise me that you will go and find yourself. Find the one you were always meant to be, the woman I see hiding inside this girl."

"I'll try."

"And one more thing," he said, running a hand down my cheek.

"Yes?" I asked.

"Let the anger go before it destroys you. After tomorrow, you walk away from all this and you don't dare look back, you hear me? Time to put down the weapons and never look back again. That's all I ask."

I nodded, and in that moment I loved him more than anyone

in my life. "I promise." We hugged tightly, two solitary figures, one family holding on by a thread under the old trees in Central Park.

"I have to go; I cannot take the risk of staying out in the open for long. Pray for me, please?" I was never very religious, but it felt like the right thing to say.

"Never stopped, dahling. Remember, four o'clock tomorrow afternoon at the theatre. Don't be late. We've only got one shot at getting you free and clear. I'll be waiting for you."

"I'll be there." I smiled at him one last time before pulling the hoodie over my head and walking away quickly. I left Richard behind, standing dead still till I was out of sight. I couldn't imagine what was going through the man's head at the moment, but I knew that I couldn't let him down again. My determination to keep my promise to him was burning brightly inside me, and after tomorrow's fatal choice . . . nothing was going to keep me from fulfilling that vow. It would be the hardest thing I had ever done in my life: putting down my weapons, letting go of my anger, and embracing peace.

Can you really do it, Charlotte? Do you possess the willpower to let it all go? The voice asked me while I hurried back to the gym. Was it testing me again, or did it already know my answer?

Yes, I can. The resolution, the conviction was clear in me. A new chapter was about to begin in my life, and I was determined to rise to the challenge. *I can do this.*

Charlotte Corday dies tomorrow.

My reemergence, my reincarnation begins tomorrow.

The last act of the huntress. This I swear.

CHAPTER THIRTY-FIVE

New York City. Decision day.

Sunday morning. I couldn't believe the day had finally arrived; it felt so surreal. I tried getting some sleep the night before but to no avail; I rolled around for hours before taping up my hands and going a few rounds with the punching bag. I poured all my frustrations and rage into the faded grey bag till the blood ran red over my white bandaged hands. Harder and harder my fists slammed into the canvas; sweat poured from my forehead, dripping down my red hair till I felt my mind starting to clear, becoming focused. I knew now what I had to do; no more doubts, no more hesitation.

One shot.

One kill.

With a final rage-filled scream, I drove my fist deep into the punching bag, leaving a gaping hole in it. I walked away as the yellow sand poured onto the cement floor, the tattered remains of the bag swinging lifelessly in the corner. I checked the Dragunov after that again; I lost count how many times. Took it apart, reassembled it almost by feel alone, cleaned it, checked the sights.

Do it again, Charlotte. You cannot afford to make a mistake. Do it again. I forced myself to focus and start the sequence again. The weapon became one in my hand, an extension of me, a lethal tool in the hands of the assassin. I stopped just before four in the morning, packing the sniper rifle away in its black metal case.

Needed to get some fresh air; the gym was starting to close in on me again as I walked out to the fire escape. A few moments later, I was sitting alone on the ledge of the brown brick building, watching the red summer sun rise over New York City. My faced was bathed in a deep orange glow as the city stirred and woke up around me. It felt like a new beginning for me; one last act and the old me could fade away. Could it really be that simple? Pull the trigger and let it all go?

Nothing is ever simple with you, Charlotte, the voice cheekily chimed in before I could hush it. My thoughts drifted to the events afterwards. Where was Richard sending me, and why was he so secretive about it? The idea of being locked in a shipping container going to God knows where didn't appeal to me, but it didn't seem like I had any choice in the matter. Over the oceans and far away I go, never to return. *What a life, Charlie, what a life.* And then for some reason, I thought back to my mother. Shouldn't I least try to say goodbye? Was she even worth it?

Probably strung out on some poor bastard's lap somewhere. Screw it; she was never there for you. I dismissed the bitch immediately from my mind and focused back on the job at hand. There was nothing more to do, all contingencies taken of, every step planned down to the very last detail. With one last look back at the early morning backdrop of the city, I hopped down from the ledge and headed back inside.

Take your time; slow it down now. I lay down in the center of the boxing ring, closing my eyes and turning the sniper rifle's cartridge over in my fingers. It was unusual, but there was an almost otherworldly calmness that had come over me. Maybe it was the power of the mask, but something inside me, a deep dark part, said that it was mostly me. The foolish girl always rushing into things was busy dying away and a calmer, more controlled woman was starting to emerge. I just had to keep it together for a little while longer. Then it would all be over.

Almost there, Charlotte, almost there. I must have lain in that ring for hours, mentally going over my plan, seeing every movement, every subtle nuance play out before my eyes. I could almost see the event unfolding before me, so real I could almost feel it. Just before one, I had a quick lunch—a simple bowl of noodles and some leftover bread from yesterday—before reaching for my bag. The Dragunov was safely tucked away inside, just waiting to be unleashed from its slumber. The last thing I did was fetch the silver mask from a box hidden under the ring. I looked at it with disdain; it was the source and bane of all my misery. I wished I had never opened the Pandora's Box in the first place, never taken the power of the Valkyrie for myself.

Too late now; best you can do is deal with it. I knew the voice was right, but I didn't say it. With one last look back at the gym, I pulled away the boards covering the door and stepped out into the world again. New York was already on the go, people bustling from place to place as I slowly made my way ever closer to the Plaza. A few clouds were drifting in from the east, casting long shadows on the pavement of the old city. A couple of tourists passed me by, caught up in their own little world, blissfully unaware of the brutal act about to play out before them. I arrived at two o'clock on the dot, buying a vanilla ice cream from a local street vendor as I surveyed the scene around me. Every exit, every escape route covered. These bastards weren't going anywhere soon; I was spinning my web ever tighter around them. Half an hour later, I checked my watch for the umpteenth time.

What if they call everything off or move the location of the meeting? A cold feeling of dread ran down my spine that all this had been for nothing, but I needn't have worried. The familiar rumble of a Lincoln Town Car sounded in the distance as I turned my back to it. Vince and the boss were early for the meeting.

Clever. Setting up the chessboard before the other players arrive, I thought, finishing up the ice cream and feeling the bulge of the Beretta in my carry bag.

Got to approach this carefully now. Vince brought three guards with him: one to cover the lower level of the parking garage, one for close protection by his side, and then a sniper providing cover from the Plaza Hotel. I will have to neutralize them first before I can make a run at the main targets, and I will have to do it quickly. Once the CEO of Venom shows up, there will be no telling how many guards he has by his side. It could turn into a goddamn turkey shoot in seconds.

You got to haul ass now, Charlotte. This party is about to go down. Gritting my teeth, I quickly moved over the street and ducked into a side entrance of the parking garage. Vince had picked his time perfectly; it was a quiet Sunday afternoon, and most of the tourists were either out in the city or catching an afternoon nap in the hotel. Stripping down in the darkness of the garage, I changed into a pair of black jeans and a grey top before reaching into my bag for the Beretta. It felt heavy in my steady left hand. When was the last time I'd used it?

The shooting at the office; I still remembered it so damn clearly. The day was burnt into my memory, there till my dying day.

Focus, bitch. You can have a trip down memory lane later, the voice scolded me as I slammed a magazine into the pistol and held it against the side of my head. The metal was cool to the touch in the gloomy, cavern-like surroundings of the garage.

This is it. Once you hit that guard, there is no going back. This is point of no return. Clicking the safety off, I took a deep sigh and nodded to myself.

Time to woman up and do this.

Slowly, I walked forward, stalking my prey like a lion on the plains of the African savannah. He never heard me appear behind him, wraithlike in my movements, soft as the gentle rains that had started falling on the streets outside, the only sound the click of a hammer and a sudden sharp intake of breath as he realized the huntress was behind him. Pulse quickening, pupils dilating, heart ripping from his chest. Did he know his end was near? Did he make his peace with whatever god he prayed to? Did it even matter in the larger scale of things?

"Remember the day you got beaten by a girl," I hissed in his ear before striking him on the jugular vein. He grunted deeply and folded in two like bad origami as I caught him by the shoulders and dragged him into a dark corner of the garage. I checked his pulse before reaching for my bag.

"*Still alive. Good.*" I was determined to keep the body count low; no killing unless absolutely necessary. Pushing him away with my foot, I looked up and listened carefully as a black limousine entered the parking garage, the car ghosting past me as I stood in the dark staring at it. Venom had arrived, and my time was running out. I had to make it to the sniper in the hotel and take him out.

All the pieces of this blood-soaked puzzle were coming together and the storm was about to break around me.

Move, Charlie! I ran from the parking garage to the hotel, breath racing as I stormed through the hotel lobby, past the shocked bellhop and up the stairs. I didn't even take notice of anybody standing around. I had to make it in time; it was my only goal.

What floor? Don't know the damn floor number. I racked my brains, taking the steps two at a time. Why was this bag so damn heavy? *Come on, think!* Then I saw it—floor thirteen. It couldn't be more ironic if it tried. Had to find the right room, but where? Come on!

Slow down and think. You can feel his heartbeat. I stopped for a moment, and I saw him at the end of the corridor, a pulsating red blob of energy radiating out. Breathing steady . . . waiting to pounce. *Not going to make it . . . Dammit, no!* Streaking down the corridor, I struck the cream-colored door with my shoulder, snapping the plywood in two as I rolled through, pistol in hand.

Only too late did I realize my mistake. *Went in too fast, didn't think it through. Overplayed my hand.* The guard had been waiting for me, smirking hideously through damaged and broken teeth as I stared down the barrel of his gun.

It's too late, Charlotte. What have you done?

A single shot rang out.

CHAPTER THIRTY-SIX

Was it all over? My thoughts dripped like water into a metallic bucket as I stared incredulously at the guard in front of me, eyes wide in shock. Was this really how my story ended? Gunshot to the head in some nondescript hotel room? It was not what I expected. No, I always thought they would find me in some garbage-filled alleyway behind a club, overdosed on heroin or some shit. Not like this. But then again, with the twists and turns my life had taken over these few months, was it really a surprise? In a way, it was almost fitting for me to go out in a blaze of violence; anything less would just not have fit the narrative of the story of my life.

The bodyguard's smile faded as his pistol fell in slow motion from his hand, bouncing off the thick green carpet. A thin trickle of blood ran down his mouth. He slumped to his knees in front of me, eyes rolling back in his head, the body dead still, a pool of scarlet forming around it as I looked up in amazement. And then I realized where the shot had come from.

Victor.

I saw my brother standing in the window of the building

across from the hotel. He flashed me a brilliant smile, lifted his sniper rifle, and turned it toward the parking garage. When I needed him the most, my brother was there for me, laying down cover fire.

"*Family, hey?*" The voice chuckled as I ran forward, flipping the bodyguard's Barrett M82 into my hands in the move. There was no time to assemble the Dragunov. I had to hope and pray the Barrett was correctly set up and calibrated.

Party's starting, kid. What you going to do? My world slowed down as the power of the Valkyrie took over. The players and the scene were perfectly laid out before my eyes, the moment frozen in time as I looked down the sights of the sniper rifle. They were all there, every one that had used and abused me, turned my life into a living hell. All there looking up at me.

The silver-haired Mafia Don. The young, blonde Venom CEO. Four bodyguards.

Vince.

Marionettes dancing on my strings. The time had come to cut one free.

Something's not right, Charlotte. Listen to me. The voice sounded in a panic, but my thoughts drowned her out, too caught up in my blind lust for vengeance. I remembered the terrible pain they both caused me, how they took my world and turned it into a mess of ashes and blood. And now it was my turn, my chance at payback.

Dammit, listen to me! The voice roared, but to no avail as I strafed the sights between the two men, taking a deep, perverted pleasure in seeing the pure terror on their faces. They turned to run as Victor dropped the first two bodyguards, two shots almost as one, heads exploding in a haze of brains and gore.

Marionettes dancing on my strings.

Panicked screams came from hotel guests far below as they ran from the hotel and into the street. My eyes never wavered from the sights, eyes steady on the prize.

Ignore them, focus on the target, block out the distractions.

Who was it going to be? The Don? Venom?

For a moment, my scope was on the Don, seeing the fat bastard trying to flee the scene. Then my mind flashed back to Venom and everything they had done to me and the others. How they destroyed innocent children's lives, all for the sake of a few power-hungry madmen sitting a million miles away in an office somewhere. I couldn't allow these monsters to carry on; I had to sever the head of the snake. It was my only choice.

My mind was made up.

"Die fucker . . ." I whispered, eyes narrowing in anger down the sight.

What happened next as I turned my scope back onto Venom, I still couldn't quite figure out, even years later. In the chaos of people running around on the roof of the parking garage, through the cacophony of Victor's shots and bodies falling to the ground, I lined up Venom, target squarely on his back, and pulled the trigger. In that exact moment, as Vince was running for cover, he collided with the Don and sent the big man straight into the path of my bullet. The .50 cartridge tore a hole clean through the Mafia boss, ripping his intestines from his body. A spray of scarlet splashed out onto the cold cement as I looked up, not daring to believe my eyes.

I didn't mean to kill you. You weren't the target, I kept thinking over and over, too numbed with shock to do anything as Venom and the last remaining guard escaped from the roof. I looked on silently as the limousine roared from the parking garage a few moments later before disappearing around the block.

Venom was gone, and my chance to finally end him had faded away.

I had failed.

Only Vince had stayed behind, kneeling next to the fallen body of the Don. He looked at his blood-soaked hands and then straightened up. Our eyes met, the massive block of a man below and the thin, lithe figure of the young girl on the balcony. His face remained emotionless, body perfectly still as he drew a bloodstained thumb over his throat. I knew instantly that I had made an enemy for life and that he would hunt me down for as long as I lived. Lowering the Barrett, I reached into the bag beside me and pulled out the silver Venom mask. Holding it tightly in my hands, I looked at the symbol of what my life had become, the very essence of my darkness. Exhaling deeply, I threw it off the balcony and watched it sail through the air before landing at Vince's feet. I didn't need it anymore, and it would be useless in his hands anyway. I was the only one with the power to unlock the dark secrets hidden inside it. And I was going to make damn sure nobody ever got their hands on it again. With one last look down at the Mafioso, hearing the blaring of incoming police sirens, the voice dragged me back to reality.

You've got to go; you can't stay here. Quickly now, Charlie. I was alone again. Even Victor had disappeared, and for a moment I wondered if it would be the last I ever saw of my brother again. I had to keep on believing that he would always be out there looking over me. *There will be time for sentimentality later. Move your ass, woman.* Moving quickly, I stripped off my black clothing and changed into a red summer dress from my bag before putting on a big pair of sunglasses and a white cloth hat. The only way I was getting out of here was with the crowd of tourists. Carefully peering through the shattered door, I saw a group of them running down the stairs, a few others banging frantically on the elevator doors. Luckily, they were in too much of a panic to notice me slipping from the wreckage of the hotel room. Putting on a terrified face, I ran toward the crowd and slipped in between them. We pushed and shoved our way down the flight of steps as I joined in enthusiastically. The hotel staff and police force tried their best to contain us, but it was an impossible task. The crowd spilled out into the lobby and through the revolving doors.

The easy part was slipping away from the hotel, the confusion and mass panic making it a piece of cake. By the time they found the bodyguard and the Dragunov upstairs, I'd be long gone. The hard part was getting to the theatre in time without being spotted.

Scores of police cars rushed past me as the chilling sound of a helicopter was heard overhead. It felt like the whole city was in a state of panic as people ran blindly past me. I could hear the fear in their voices as they shouted at each other: "It's the Huntress; it has to be her! We got to get out of here!" I kept my cool; I mean who would ever suspect the young lady with the summer dress and big hat to be a homicidal maniac? I moved silently with the crowd till I managed to duck into a nearby alley. Only then, once I could catch my breath again, did the full extent of what I'd just done sink in.

You killed the head of the Italian Mafia in New York City. They will swear a blood oath and come after you with everything they got. They won't stop till you are six feet under the ground. Any thoughts of staying in New York after all this was over had vanished the instant I pulled that trigger. Vince and the upper echelons of the Cosa Nostra would never forgive me for what I'd done. There would be no redemption, no mercy if they ever caught up with me. I couldn't even think of the horrific acts and torture that were waiting if I ever dared set foot in the city again.

You got to keep moving, Charlie. Time's running out.

The events at the Plaza had taken longer than I anticipated, and I was running behind schedule. If I missed the boat . . . No, I couldn't think like that. I picked myself up and dragged my tired body forward, constantly checking my watch for the time.

Twenty to four . . . Damn . . . going to be late. The theatre was still a few blocks away and I knew the odds of me getting spotted increased with every minute I was out in the open. Flying past a television store, I saw the news bulletin flashing across the numerous screens. The hunt for the Huntress had resumed, and the NYPD had already locked down the airports and train stations. Nobody was getting in or out of the city without their say so, and it wouldn't be long before the ports were closed as well. The net was closing tighter around me, my chances of escape growing less by the second.

Come on, Charlotte, almost there . . . Just a little bit further. Breaking out into a full sprint, I ran the last two blocks in record time. Then, finally, I saw the Winter Gardens Theatre appearing before me in the distance. Richard and Peter were already waiting for me, pacing nervously around a beat-up old Ford Mustang SVO. I could see the relief in Richard's face as I ran up and jumped in his arms, hugging him tightly. I looked back at Peter, who smiled sadly, said nothing, and climbed into the passenger seat.

"My God, dahling, we didn't think you were going to make it. Was it you at the Plaza Hotel or should I not ask?" Richard was nearly mad with worry as he held me by the shoulders.

"It's a long story. Are we ready to go?" I asked, trying to catch my breath again.

"All set, dear. Just waiting on you. What in the name of Aretha Franklin's titties are you wearing?! Oh, this will simply not do for a long sea journey. I got you a set of clothes for emergencies. Go get dressed inside and hurry; the ship is leaving soon," replied Richard, bundling me into the theatre. Two minutes later I reappeared, dressed in faded blue jeans and an old Giants jersey.

"Better?"

"Anything is better than that disaster you had on. Now hop in. We will have to move our delightful fannies if we are going to make it in time." Richard jumped in the driver's seat while I scurried into the back seat, trying to calm my racing heart.

We were finally off, the Mustang wheezing and puffing mightily as we left the theatre and my old life behind.

The destination? Unknown.

The next chapter in my epic story was about to begin, far and away across the wide, blue ocean. One girl on a fantastic journey, leaving a city in flames behind, a place she could never come back to.

And somewhere on a balcony, Vince stood watching out on the great metropolis as the sun set behind him, cigarette hanging from his fingers. A wicked if subtle smile formed on his face as he lifted a snifter of fine Spanish brandy to his lips and downed it slowly before turning and walking back into his penthouse apartment.

EPILOGUE

The little red Mustang sped on, leaving Manhattan behind in its wake. I suddenly felt so tired; the adrenaline was gone from my body. The events of the past few hours had finally caught up with me as my head slumped backwards on the faded yellow leather seats of the car. I didn't want to think of everything that had taken place in my life these past few months, but it was difficult not to. Going from a strung-out addict to a fleeing refugee from my own country, it was difficult to believe at times that all this had happened to me. I thought back to that fateful first night when I killed those thugs in the alleyway, when I realized there was something different, something not human to me. And then my mind drifted to Vince and how he had taken care of me, was always around when I needed him.

God, has he already started the hunt for me? For the one that took down the boss of one of the most powerful and evil organizations in the world? The words never truly made sense to me; it was too unbelievable to completely grasp and understand. I had committed one of the most unforgivable acts imaginable, and I wondered how long it would take them to come after me.

Let it go, Charlotte. There is nothing you can do about it now. Pushing it to the back of my mind, I looked over at Peter sitting quietly in the passenger seat. He kept looking out into the distance, not saying a word or even making eye contact. I remembered how I met him and Richard, how they trusted me and took me into their home. They even shared their darkest secret hidden away in the basement of the salon. I put them through an unimaginable hell and yet they stood by me—through everything, I was never forsaken by them. Though it was killing me to see Peter like this, I just wished there was something . . . anything I could say to him to make up for what I had done.

I put my hand on his shoulder. "Peter?" But he shrugged it off without a word and continued to gaze aimlessly at the buildings rolling by. Richard looked back at me in the rearview mirror and shook his head softly. I knew he was telling me to let it go and it was not the right time to push the issue. I sat quietly back in the seat and closed my eyes, letting the world drift by me. It was the first time I was able relax in what must have been days, if not weeks. Sunday evening jazz floated out from the old Pioneer car radio, often interrupted by another news report. The whole city was in a state of panic, and the mayor had just announced a strict curfew and that everyone had to stay indoors. Some idiot out in a far borough swore he saw the Huntress in New Jersey, and he was convinced she was coming for him and his family. I shut out the reporter's blathering as Richard calmly but firmly switched off the radio.

"I think that's quite enough of that. Anyway, we're only fifteen minutes away from the docks. Open the back seat; there should be a small duffle bag inside. I packed you some extra clothing for the trip." I folded down the seat and fished inside the trunk before pulling out a black cloth bag and putting it next to me. As promised, a few minutes later we arrived at the docks, the Mustang pulling up to a dilapidated guard station. A heavyset man with a grey moustache wandered out with a clipboard in his hands. He saw Richard in the driver's seat and nodded at him.

"Pier 54, over by the far side. Everything is ready and waiting for you. Careful, the cops are already here, but we managed to keep them off you for a bit; told them there was hazardous material being loaded over there. Good luck." He smiled, nodding and lifting the boom gate. He caught a glimpse of me in the back seat, and I could see the flicker of recognition in his rapidly widening eyes. Before he could say or do anything, the Mustang rolled past him in the direction of the far docks. Our luck held out—it was Sunday and the docks were relatively deserted. There were only a few dock workers standing idly and a couple police cars some distance away from us. Nobody even took notice of the little red Mustang in their midst. We quietly slipped deeper into the dockyards, searching for the correct pier and ship till we finally found it—the *SS Empire Maersk,* a great, hulking container ship that had seen better days in its life. It looked like it was held together by rust and good intentions alone, but it would have to do. A thin man with greying hair and a sea captain's hat on was waiting by an open cargo container, tapping his feet impatiently. With a puff of dust, the Mustang pulled up and we got out.

"Christ, you took your sweet time, didn't you? You know

how difficult it is to convince those assholes in blue to stay away from this area? Hazardous materials my ass; it's a shipment of tuna cans for God's sake," he fumed, wiping the sweat off his brow with a dirty brown rag while looking around nervously.

Richard smiled, patting the man on the shoulder. "Relax the tits, dahling, I told you we would be on time, didn't I?" He turned and motioned for me to come closer before introducing me. "This is Frank, a distant cousin of mine. He often helps to smuggle in some of our more exotic hair care products. Frank, this is the young lady I was telling you about. Are we all set to go?"

"You are asking a damn lot of me, you know that? Weapons are one thing, but human cargo? If the cops catch us doing this, we'll all rot in the slammer for the rest of our natural damn lives," the plank wailed, folding his skipper's hat back and forth in his hands.

"I wouldn't ask if it wasn't important, and besides, you owe me from that score you made last Christmas. How much was it again? Refresh my memory, dear. Now, I trust you have everything in order like I asked?" Richard cooed wickedly, knowing that he had the man in the palm of his hand.

"Christ . . . Yeah, I got everything. There is enough food and water in there for two weeks, more than enough for her trip; it shouldn't take more than a week anyway. I also had some holes cut in the side for oxygen and I even included a damn bucket and a flashlight," Frank replied with a sag of the shoulders, shaking his head in disbelief.

"And the passport?" Richard asked, flashing a brilliant smile in Frank's direction.

"This took some doing, let me tell you that. I had to kiss so much ass and fondle so many pockets for this . . . Here." He handed over a small black book as Richard nodded and tapped him softly on the head with it.

"Good boy. Now give me a moment with the young lady please?"

"Just hurry up, for the love of mercy, okay? My balls are hanging out on this one, and I don't like it one fucking bit." My uncle ignored his rant and turned to me, handing the passport over.

"That's the last bit of the puzzle dear; you are all set to go." I could see a small tear was already forming in one eye as he held me by the shoulders.

"Just exactly where are you sending me?" I asked suspiciously, eyeing the small felt-covered book in my hand.

Richard bit his lip like a child that had been caught with his hands in the cookie jar and whispered into my ear. I stepped back in total shock, thinking he was joking with me.

"What?!" I exclaimed, not believing what I just heard. "Why in the world would you even think of sending me there?"

"It's the last place anyone would ever think of looking for you, dahling, and besides, Cousin Mickey said he would take good care of you for as long as it takes. He might seem a bit off now and again, but he is a fabulous type and I trust him."

"You've been inhaling too much hair spray lately." I laughed, trying to fight back the tears as I hugged him tightly.

"Maybe so, dear, maybe so. You ready to go?" he asked, rubbing my shoulders in comfort.

"I have one more thing to do. Just give me a moment please." I rushed over to Peter, who was standing by the car, looking out over the water. He never had a chance to protest as I wrapped my arms around him. "I'm sorry for everything. Please forgive me?"

He nodded, and I could see tears in his eyes as well. "Good luck, sweetie. I'll send you some biscuits when I can."

With a last look back at my uncle, I waved goodbye and walked over to Richard. "Now I'm ready to go." I placed a large metal object in his hands, folding his fingers around it and nodding at him. It was the Beretta. I still hadn't let go of it since the events at the Plaza, keeping it safe in a thigh holster on my leg.

"Take it and throw it into the deepest part of the ocean you can find. I won't need it anymore." I kissed Richard on the forehead and headed into the waiting container. Sighing deeply, I watched Frank close the doors. My uncles faded from view and I was alone again, the surrounding darkness my only friend.

Farewell, New York. Into the unknown I go.

Eight days later, somewhere over the Atlantic Ocean.

It had been the worst, most miserable week of my entire life. Seasick as hell from the rocking of the container ship, I had puked my guts out for the first three days of the voyage. I spent most of the time lying on my side, clutching my stomach in agony and trying to get some sleep. This proved impossible, the constant pounding and roaring of the waves slamming against the ship, tossing me around in the container. And if I had to see another can of fucking Spam and baked beans, it would have been my end. I would have killed myself just on general principal about it. The worst thing, though, was using the bucket. I had wondered why Frank included it in the container in the first place. Within a day, the reality had dawned on me, the smell driving me to near insanity.

I had begun to lose my mind during the long days of the journey, cramped up in the confining closeness of the metal container. I tried to conserve the flashlight's battery, but it soon ran out and I was wrapped in darkness again. I even had a long discussion about the Yankees with the voice in my head. Turned out it was a Mets supporter, to make matters worse. I was on the verge of devising a plan to commit suicide with a water bottle when I felt the ship lurching to a halt. The mighty diesel engines fell silent, and everything settled down again. I could just make out the distant whine of a crane, then the uneasy sensation of the container being lifted up into the air and placed on the ground with a metallic thud. Someone was fiddling with the locks of the container while I backed into the farthest and darkest corner possible. The doors swung open, and bright sunshine flooded into the space, blinding me for a few moments. I saw the silhouette of a man standing in the door, a mop of scraggy brown hair framing his face. His voice was deep and rich, commanding immediate attention as he looked me over.

"Well, fook me, you must be Charlotte. Damn glad to finally meet you . . . You look like the ass end of hell, though, lassie."

"Who . . . who are you? Where am I?" I was heavily disorientated from the long sea journey and feeling very unsteady on my feet as the strong hands folded over mine and lifted me to my feet.

He flashed me a fantastically handsome smile, folding his tattooed-covered arms and winking at me. "The name's Michael O'Donnell, but you can call me Cousin Mickey. Welcome to Northern Ireland."

END

ABOUT THE AUTHOR

John Murray McKay is a parts unknown writer specializing in the genres of fantasy, historical, and science fiction. He started off in writing by penning the long-running web series Man on an Island that ran for multiple years. He finds his inspiration in the works of authors like Clive Cussler and in filmmakers like Quentin Tarantino. His critically acclaimed debut novel, *The N Days,* took him into the dark heart of a postapocalyptic USA, and now he returns to the Red, White, and Blue with his second series, The Venom Protocols. By day, he plies his trade as an English and Social Science teacher at a local primary school. John resides in Pretoria, South Africa, but hopes to move to the United States of America soon to further his career as an author. He has a dog, two rescue cats, and a beard that he currently takes care of.

CHECK OUT OTHER WORKS FROM CORVUS QUILL PRESS LLC

The Girl's Guide To The Apocalypse
John Murray McKay

Dark Dimensions
J.A. Duxbury

Shadows and a Touch Of Magic
S.E. Cyborski

9 781736 207550